Torrie & the Pirate-Queen

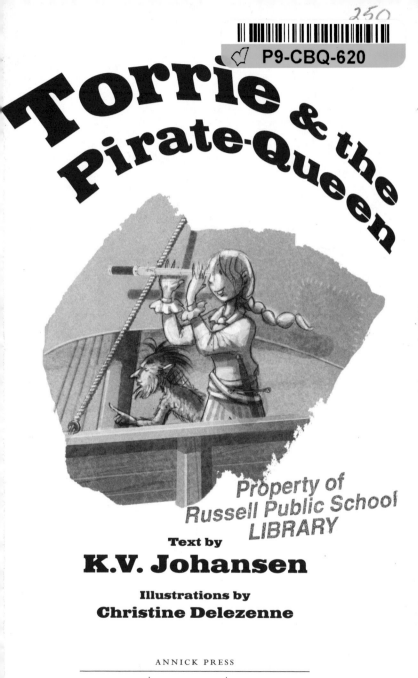

Text by

K.V. Johansen

Illustrations by

Christine Delezenne

ANNICK PRESS

TORONTO + NEW YORK + VANCOUVER

Text © 2005 K.V. Johansen
Illustrations © 2005 Christine Delezenne

Annick Press Ltd.

We acknowledge the support of the Canada Council for the Arts, the Ontario Arts Council,
and the Government of Canada through the Book Publishing Industry Development Program
(BPIDP) for our publishing activities.

Edited by Pam Robertson
Copy edited by Elizabeth McLean
Cover design and interior design by Irvin Cheung/iCheung Design
Cover and interior illustrations by Christine Delezenne

The text was typeset in Perpetua and Egyptienne

Cataloging in Publication
Johansen, K.V. (Krista V.), 1968–
       Torrie and the pirate queen / written by K.V. Johansen;
illustrated by Christine Delezenne.

ISBN 1-55037-901-1 (bound).—ISBN 1-55037-900-3 (pbk.)

I. Delezenne, Christine II. Title.

PS8569.O2676T675 2005   jC813'.54   C2004-905911-4

Printed and bound in Canada

Published in the U.S.A. by	**Distributed in Canada by**	**Distributed in the U.S.A. by**
Annick Press (U.S.) Ltd.	Firefly Books Ltd.	Firefly Books (U.S.) Inc.
	66 Leek Crescent	P.O. Box 1338
	Richmond Hill, ON	Ellicott Station
	L4B 1H1	Buffalo, NY 14205

Visit our website at **www.annickpress.com**

for April,
who wanted a book
about Anna

CHAPTER ONE

In which Anna fights a duel

This is a story about a heroic sea captain, and an enchanted treasure, and pirates. It happened long ago in the days of Queen Dendroica the First of Erythroth, granddaughter of my friends, the great dragon-killers Rufik and Cossypha. It begins on the coast of the kingdom of Erythroth with Anna, a young sea captain and master mariner. She was sitting on the end of a wharf with a sword on her lap, swinging her legs and frowning out over the sea, deep in thought.

Anna was tall and lean and tanned. I could tell she spent all her time out in the sun and the wind. I could tell she was strong, probably from hauling at ropes and wrestling with the tiller during storms. She had a mass of glossy black hair, which was supposed to be in a pigtail, the way sailors always wore it in those days, but it was so curly it kept springing out. One of her eyes was blue and the other one was green, but they were both

the color of the ocean. When she smiled she had dimples, but right then she wasn't smiling at all. She was holding a sheathed sword across her lap, as I said, turning it over and over. Every now and then she stopped and bit the end of her long braid in a thoughtful manner.

"What do I do?" she asked, and she looked at the fluffy, mostly white collie dog that was sitting beside her. She wasn't really asking the dog, of course. Humans can't talk to dogs. She was just thinking out loud. "What do I do, Yah-Yah? Should I challenge Mister Flytch to a duel?"

The dog whined as though she didn't like the idea.

"I can't think of any other way," said Anna. "I need that ship. There's no other way to do what I have to do. And anyhow, she's my ship. My grandfather left her to me when he died." She drew the sword a little and looked at the light gleaming on the silvery blade. "So, if Flytch won't give her to me, I'll have to take her."

The dog whined again. Anna patted her and jumped up, flicking her pigtail over her shoulder.

"Yes, you're right, Yah-Yah," she said. "We've wasted enough time, and we've got responsibilities. Mister Flytch isn't going to boss me about my own ship—I'll do it."

She fastened the sword to her belt and strode back along the wharf.

The dog whimpered and ran after her.

There was just one ship tied up at the wharf, a dark, tarry ship that looked as if she had seen more than her fair share of storms and battles. And if you're going to listen to my tale, you need to know that for real sailors, a ship is always a she. The flag that fluttered from her masthead was black, and on it in white was a bird perched on a skull. The name painted across the stern was *Shrike*, which is a sort of bird that hangs its prey up on thorns, like meat on hooks in a butcher's shop. A handful of tough-looking old sailors sat on the deck in the sun. Some of them were peeling potatoes, and two were gutting fish.

"Hullo, Anna dear," said one of the potato-peelers. "Back from your walk so soon?"

"Don't you call me 'dear,' Flytch," Anna said sternly. "I've come to challenge you."

"Challenge me?" asked the man, raising his bushy black eyebrows. "*Me?*"

"Yes," said Anna. "You. You're the one refusing to take my orders. You're the one refusing to give me my ship."

"She's not your ship, dear," said Mister Flytch.

"Yes, she is, and you know it," said Anna. "Before my grandfather Lanius died, he gave me his sword and told me that *Shrike* was to be mine, too, once I was old enough. Well, I'm old enough now. I've been my father's apprentice on his ship *Oriole* for seven years and I've come to claim *Shrike* the way my grandfather wanted."

"But we need *Shrike*, dear, for fishing."

"Fishing! You, the crew of Captain Lanius, fishing! You used to be the terror of the seas!"

"We've retired," said Mister Flytch.

"I don't care," said Anna. "*I* need *Shrike*."

"You can't have her," he said. "Now go home, dear."

Anna drew her sword.

"Make me," she said.

"It was nice of you to visit us, Anna. Now go home."

"I don't have a home," said Anna. "Just my ship. I'm not afraid to fight for her. Are you?"

One of the other sailors, a thin, wiry woman with white hair in a fat pigtail and a rather pretty, pointy face, like an elderly pixie, chuckled and elbowed Mister Flytch in the ribs. He turned brick red with outrage.

"Me?" he roared. "Afraid? Of you? I was first mate to Captain Lanius, the terror of the seas!"

"Yes," said Anna, very sweetly. "And now you are just an old, grouchy fisherman. But I am the granddaughter of Captain Lanius, and *Shrike* is mine!"

She jumped down to the deck of the ship.

Mister Flytch leapt to his feet. He was a big, dark man, broad-shouldered and tall, and though he was bald, his beard was still bristly and black. "Mirimick!" he bellowed. "My sword!"

The pigtailed woman darted away. In a moment she was back with a sword. It was a very old, battered, well-used-looking sword. But so was Anna's, and hers wasn't rusty.

"I'll give you one last chance, Mister Flytch," said Anna. "Give—me—my—ship."

"No," said Mister Flytch, and then the swords rang together with a noise like jangling bells.

The other sailors hurried to move their pot of potatoes and

fish out of the way, and more men and women came scrambling up the ladder from the hold, until there were about twelve of them standing along the rail, watching. There wasn't one of them who didn't have gray hair or wrinkles, but they all looked tough and hard, and they all had knives in their belts or boot-tops, at least those who were wearing boots. Many of them were barefoot.

Mister Flytch was big and strong, but Anna was nimble and fast. She dodged his every lunge and slash and darted around him like a dragonfly, now here, now there, her sword a flicker of bright steel. No matter how fast she was, though, his blade always met hers. Once she caught the flat of his sword on her own and twisted it somehow so that it spun away clattering along the deck. Some of the sailors cheered, but Mister Flytch dove after it and stood up again, sword in hand. Most of the sailors cheered for him. Yah-Yah the dog growled. Flytch charged at Anna and she stepped aside, turning to face him as he turned. He was beginning to sweat and puff for breath, but he advanced again, slow and menacing, looking like a big black bull, angry and dangerous, forcing Anna back towards the rail where she wouldn't be able to dance around him.

Then Anna suddenly yelled and lunged straight for him. The old first mate jumped backwards away from her, and instead of landing on his feet he seemed to trip in the air. He landed sprawling on his back with a great "whoosh" of breath. His weapon flew clattering away, and Anna stood with the tip of her sword resting on his throat. Most of the watching sailors groaned. A few clapped their hands.

"Do you yield, Mister Flytch?" Anna asked sternly, panting for breath herself.

"Oh, my back," he moaned. "I'm getting too old for this."

"You're only as old as you feel, Flytch," the pixie-ish woman he had called Mirimick said cheerfully. She had been one of the ones clapping for Anna.

"Mister Flytch," said Anna. "Whose ship is this?"

Mister Flytch crossed his eyes so as to focus on the sword so near his nose. "Yours," he said. "Captain."

He sat up on the deck, rubbing his back with one hand and wiping the dripping sweat from his face with the other. "Yours," he said again, and sighed. "I've lived almost my whole life on this ship. I'll hate to leave her."

"Who said you had to leave her?" asked Anna. "I need a first mate, Mister Flytch." She looked at the thin, white-haired woman. "And I need a bow master, Mirimick. I need a crew. We're sailing into hostile waters."

The sailors began to look more cheerful.

"Did you think I wanted her for a houseboat?" Anna asked. "There's some business I have to settle, with an enemy of my grandfather's. I need *Shrike* to do it. But I need you, too, if you'll have me as captain and accept my orders."

Mister Flytch started to get to his feet, slowly and carefully. Anna gave him a hand up.

"Sir," he said. "*Shrike* is yours, and so is her crew. What are your orders?"

"Lay in provisions for a long voyage," said Anna. "We're sailing to the South Seas."

"The South Seas? Aye aye, sir," said Mister Flytch. He sounded quite eager. I suppose the old pirates were beginning to find retirement a bit boring, and that was why even Flytch seemed so happy to let Anna take command, without asking any more questions about where they were going and why. The first mate began giving orders to the rest of the crew, about salting down the last catch of fish, and laying in supplies of water and ship's biscuit and salt beef and sauerkraut, which are the sorts of foods that last for a long time at sea. I think maybe part of the reason they last is that people get very tired of all that salty stuff and don't eat so much.

Anna looked all around to make certain the sailors weren't watching. Then she walked over to the foot of the mast. Yah-Yah followed her, and the dog looked up and growled. Anna was looking up, too.

"I don't know what you are," she said, standing there with the sun gleaming on her blade. "But you can climb down out of my rigging right now. I saw you trip poor old Flytch."

And Yah-Yah the dog growled deep in her chest.

I decided to stay right where I was, safely up the mast.

Chapter Two

In which
I go to sea

Before I tell you any more about Anna, I'd better tell you a little about myself, because I'm in the story too. I'm not saying I'm the hero—it's really Anna who is the hero of this tale, though I did a few heroic things along the way—but even though I'm not the hero, I'm in it, so you'd better know who I am.

I'm Torrie. Not *a* Torrie, but *the* Torrie. There's only one of me. I'm the oldest of the Old Things of the Wild Forest, and the cleverest, even if I do say so myself. I've lived in the Wild Forest for hundreds and hundreds of years, and I expect I'll go on living there for hundreds and hundreds more, except when I get restless and go off on an adventure, which happens from time to time.

I'm not very big, only about three feet tall. I have long, slender fingers and toes, and nice, big, pointy ears, sharp lit-

tle fangs like a fox, brilliant yellow eyes, a very handsome nose (which isn't too large at all, whatever some people may say), and I'm covered all over in shaggy, rust-colored fur. I don't bother with clothes at all. That's a human thing.

Now, you may not know much about us Old Things. Most humans don't, any more. We Old Things come in dozens of kinds, but there are a few traits we have in common. We're all magical, some more so and some less, of course. Generally, humans can only see us when we want them to, which comes in very handy, as you'll find out. We can talk to animals—actually, some of my best friends are animals. And we hate the touch of iron. We're old—old as the oldest humans, older than iron tools and weapons, and maybe that's why. Some say we belong to the old days, when human men and women used stone and bronze and believed in us Old Things more than they do now. I don't know if that's true or not, I just know iron and steel give me a rash.

The only weapon I have is my spear, and its point isn't iron, but beautiful, gleaming bronze. It's very useful against things like goblins and dragons.

I'd come down to the little fishing village of Queen's Harbor in the kingdom of Erythroth because there hadn't been much exciting happening in the Wild Forest that spring, and my feet were itchy. That happens sometimes. I get itchy feet and I have to go off wandering until I find an adventure, or an adventure finds me. I can tell, just a feeling in the air, like the first sniff of autumn frost, when I'm close to adventure. I'd been beginning to think I was wrong about Queen's Harbor, though, because so far there had been no adventure there at all. The most exciting thing in the village was a ship full of retired pirates working as fishermen. I'd been about to leave when things got exciting at last: Anna showed up and told Mister Flytch that she wanted the ship. They had argued a lot, she had said she was going for a walk, and then she had gone to sit on the end of the wharf to think, before going back and challenging him to a duel, which is where the whole adventure began.

Anyway, when Anna and Mister Flytch the first mate began fighting, I was right there on the ship watching. None of the humans could see me, and I tried to keep in the shadows so the dog wouldn't notice—some animals are good at seeing or smelling us Old Things, whether we want them to or not. I was a bit worried. I could tell Anna and Mister Flytch didn't really want to hurt one another, but I could also see that each wanted very badly to win the duel. And they were both outstanding swordsmen. Or swordswomen. I mean, one was one and one was the other ....

Well, whichever they were, I knew when they started fighting that I had to do something. It would all turn into a tragedy, if Anna or Mister Flytch was wounded or even killed in the duel. And of course Anna had to win, because if she didn't, she wouldn't be able to take *Shrike* out to sea—and I had already decided to go to sea with her. That was the adventure I was smelling.

So when I saw the mate jump backwards I jumped myself and grabbed him around the ankles so that he fell flat on his back. And then I scrambled up the mast out of the way. But Anna saw me. I suppose it was because I was thinking about her so much that I made myself visible to her, even though I hadn't meant to, not right then.

〰〰〰〰〰

"Good morning," I said to Anna, as she stood there, frowning up at me.

"What are you?" Anna asked, and she waved her sword at me in a way that made me decide to stay right where I was.

"It's a brownie," the dog said, and she growled.

"I am not a brownie!" I said. "Brownies are smaller than me, and not so handsome and furry. They live around farmhouses and help with the chores if you give them milk, and I certainly don't help with the chores, although I am quite fond of milk. I'm Torrie."

Anna raised one eyebrow at me, as if she doubted what I had said. "What's a Torrie?"

"Me," I said. "Not *a* Torrie. *The* Torrie. I'm the only one there is."

"Why did you trip Mister Flytch?"

"I wanted you to win before you had to hurt him," I said. "I'm going to sea with you."

"No, you're not!"

"Yes, I am," I said. "You need my help."

"No, I don't. And you don't even know why I'm going to sea."

"Because you're a sailor," I said, playing for time while I thought. "That's obvious. Sailors have to go to sea."

Anna snorted, trying not to laugh, and opened her mouth. Probably she was about to say something sarcastic. It had been a rather foolish thing for me to say.

"And," I said hastily, "there's something you have to do. Something important. You need the ship to do it." I had guessed that much from what she said to the dog.

Anna shut her mouth again, looking thoughtful.

"Don't listen to him," said the dog, showing me her teeth. "It's a trick. I wouldn't trust him any more than I'd trust these pirates. You can rescue your father without his help, whatever he calls himself."

"You're going to rescue your father," I said, and winked at the dog. "It's a sort of a quest. You see, that's why you need my help. I'm good at quests. I've been on lots of them. Quests and adventures, that's what I'm good at."

"How did you know that?" Anna asked.

"Well, I've been on lots of quests and adventures, and I've always survived," I said. "So I must be good at them."

"I mean," she said carefully, "how did you know about my father? I haven't even told the crew yet."

I suppose I could have pretended it was magic but that wouldn't have been honest, and if we were going to be friends, I had to be honest.

"Actually, your dog mentioned it," I said. "Umm, if you could get her to stop growling at me, I might come down."

"Quiet, Yah-Yah," Anna said, sheathing her sword, and I climbed down the mast. Once I had my feet on the deck I bowed grandly.

"Torrie," I said. "Master Adventurer, at your service, Captain."

"Don't be silly," she said, but she smiled, showing the dimples in her cheeks.

Yah-Yah snorted. "Anna doesn't need you."

"That's what you think," I said.

"What?" asked Anna.

"Yah-Yah says you don't need me. She's jealous. And she doesn't like your crew, either."

Anna threw back her head and laughed. "I knew that. They're my grandfather Lanius's crew. They used to be pirates, like him. She always used to growl at my grandfather, too."

The crew were all hurrying around us now, organizing things. They were giving Anna some funny looks, but not one said anything about her apparently talking to her dog. She was the captain, after all.

"They can't see you, can they?" Anna asked, and began to bite the end of her pigtail, which I was beginning to realize was a sign she was debating something in her mind.

"Not unless I want them to."

Anna tapped her chin with the end of the braid, which she still held, but all she said was, "Hmm."

"No," Yah-Yah growled. "Pirates are bad enough. What would your father say? You don't need a brownie."

"I'm not a brownie," I said again. "I told you."

"Yah-Yah, be nice to him," said Anna. "Stop growling. All right, Torrie, you can come with me."

"Thank you, Captain," I said. We shook hands.

"Shake, Yah-Yah," Anna ordered, and Yah-Yah reluctantly gave me a paw.

"Now," I said. "Tell me all about your quest. Your father is missing?"

"My father is a prisoner," Anna said grimly.

"I'm good at rescues. I rescued a crown prince, once."

"Well, my father's not a crown prince. He's a master mariner, a sea captain."

"A pirate?" I asked.

"No!" said Anna.

"Certainly not!" Yah-Yah growled. "Captain Icterus is a decent, honest merchant, not like his father, Lanius the pirate Captain Icterus would never want Anna to sail with this crew, never."

"Is Yah-Yah saying rude things about my grandfather?" Anna asked.

"Sort of," I admitted. It was easy for even a human to see she was, actually, because of the way her lips pulled back from her fangs.

"I liked my grandfather, even if he was a pirate," Anna said. "So there. Anyhow, Yah-Yah, where else am I going to get a ship and a crew, tell me that?"

Yah-Yah couldn't, of course.

"So who's holding your father prisoner?" I asked, while

Yah-Yah grumbled to herself about smelly old pirates.

"It's a long story," Anna cautioned.

"I like long stories."

"Let's get off the ship first, before Flytch decides I've gone mad. If he sees me talking to invisible creatures, he might refuse to sail with me after all. Unless you'd like to let them see you."

A dozen pirates, I thought. I wasn't ready to have a dozen pirates knowing I existed, not until I got to know them a bit better. Some people, like Anna, I just feel I know at once, as though we've been friends forever the moment I lay eyes on them. Others, well, it takes time to learn what sort of people they really are.

"Not yet," I said. "I'll wait till I know them better."

Anna and Yah-Yah and I went back to the end of the wharf, where we could talk with a little privacy from the ship.

"My grandfather, Captain Lanius, was a pirate," Anna began. "And a long time ago he raided the palace of Queen Nevilla and stole a treasure."

"Queen Nevilla!" I yelped. "The pirate-queen?"

I had heard quite a few stories about Queen Nevilla, even in the Wild Forest, far from the sea. She had raided the palace of the Sultan of Callipepla and stolen the crown jewels. She had kidnapped the Crown Princess of High Morroway and kept her locked in a dungeon for six months, until her father the king paid an enormous ransom. The poor princess had nothing but rice and seaweed soup to eat the whole time. And there were dozens of other tales about people Nevilla had taken hostage or ships she'd captured.

"Yes, the pirate-queen," Anna said. "Nevilla's the Queen of the Granite Isles, and the Granite Islanders are all pirates. They attack ships and steal their cargoes to sell themselves. Sometimes they hold wealthy passengers hostage until their relatives pay huge ransoms."

"And your grandfather managed to steal a treasure from Nevilla herself?" I was impressed. "Did the queen steal the treasure back?"

"No. My grandfather buried it, someplace so secret that even his crew don't know where it is. And Queen Nevilla never found it, although she's been looking for it for forty years. My family has always kept well away from the Granite Isles, because the pirate-queen would do anything to get that treasure back."

"It must be an exciting treasure, then," I said. "Heaps of gold and jewels. Or maybe a magic sword. Or a wishing lamp. Or a ring of invisibility. Or maybe a golden egg, and when you open it there's a whole world inside, and …"

"I don't know," Anna interrupted, tapping me on the head. "Let me finish. It doesn't matter what it is. The important thing is that last fall my father's ship, *Oriole*, was caught in a hurricane and blown off course. And they ended up in the Granite Isles. Queen Nevilla's ships captured them and locked my father and his crew in her dungeon, and she won't let them out until my father tells her where Grandfather Lanius hid the treasure."

"Why doesn't he tell her, then?" I asked. It sounded perfectly simple to me.

"Because he doesn't know where the treasure is," Anna

explained. "My grandfather never told anyone. Except me, when I was a little girl."

"Aha," I said. I thought about that. "Um ... Anna, how come you weren't captured, too? You said you were your father's apprentice."

Anna scowled, almost as though she were embarrassed. "I had an accident last summer. During a storm I fell and broke my leg. So I was staying with my uncle in the capital when *Oriole* left on that voyage."

"Aha," I said again. "Umm ... so how come you know what happened to *Oriole*?"

"*I* was a prisoner too," said Yah-Yah. "*I* escaped. They didn't bother guarding a dog. Captain Icterus wrote a letter and put it in a waterproof oilcloth pouch and tied it to my collar. Then I escaped. Heroically." She gave me a *so there* sort of look, ears pricked up and tongue hanging out of her grinning mouth. "I stowed away on a smuggler's ship to get back to the mainland, and then I stowed away on a merchant ship, to come back to the north, and then I walked, for months and months and months, to get home to Erythroth and find Anna."

"Yah-Yah escaped and brought me a letter from my father," said Anna, who of course hadn't heard Yah-Yah saying the same thing. She ruffled up the dog's fur and smiled at her. "She was very heroic."

"Yes," I said. "She was just telling me. So what are we going to do?"

"I'm going to sail to the South Seas and find my grandfather's treasure," said Anna. "Once I have it I can make Nevilla the

pirate-queen free my father and his ship and his crew. Unless," and she started fiddling with the end of her braid again, although she didn't actually begin nibbling at it this time, "unless it turns out there's some better way to rescue them. Some way where someone invisible might be useful. Because if Nevilla gets that treasure back, she wins, and my grandfather would never have wanted her to win."

"Oh," I said, but what I thought was, well, it was Queen Nevilla's treasure in the first place, wasn't it? But Anna's grandfather was a pirate, and I guess she couldn't help thinking like one sometimes.

Yah-Yah and I looked at one another, and for once we agreed about something.

"We'll talk her out of it," said the dog, laying her ears back. "Let the queen have her silly old treasure."

"So long as we get to find it first," I said. "Finding treasure is something else I'm good at."

"What are you two talking about?" Anna asked suspiciously.

"Nothing," I said. "Nothing at all. When do we leave?"

"As soon as the ship is ready."

"Good," I said. "I've never been to sea before. I'm looking forward to a nice relaxing sea voyage."

Little did I know then, just how *un*relaxing that voyage was going to be.

Chapter Three

In which there is a storm

Y ou'd probably like to know a little more about the ship, since she's so important to the story. *Shrike* was a type of vessel called a cog, which was very common in those days. She had a mainmast with a big square sail, which was blood red, so that people would find it frightening, and a mizzenmast. That means a mast at the back—and we sailors call the back the "stern" and the front the "bow." The mizzenmast had a lateen sail, which is sort of pointy and hung slantwise, and if you still don't understand you'll just have to go look it up. The lateen sail was white, because they didn't have enough red canvas.

Shrike had a forecastle and an aftercastle, for fighting from. These were raised sections, almost like little towers or buildings, in the bow and stern. That's why they call them "castles." When *Shrike* was in a battle, Mirimick the bow master would send her archers or crossbowmen up on top of the castles, so they could fire down onto the decks of the other ship. For turning the rudder, *Shrike* had a big heavy tiller under the aftercastle. It took six large sailors to hold the tiller steady when there was a storm. And there was a big firebox full of sand for making a fire on, to cook, which meant that whenever the seas were rough we ate cold food, because of the danger of the fire getting loose. The hold was full of casks of water, which tasted sort of tired and swampy after a few weeks, and barrels of things like hard ship's biscuit, sauerkraut, limes, onions, salt beef, pickles, oatmeal, and of course potatoes for making fish chowder, which was the pirates' favorite food.

I LIKED BEING AT SEA, even though it did mean eating fish chowder at least once every day. Yah-Yah and I hunted rats among the barrels and the ballast-stones, and I tried to stay out of the way of the pirates. Them not being able to see me was all very well, but they could still trip over me. At night, Anna and I would sit on top of the forecastle looking down at the water and up at the stars, and Anna would tell me about the strange and distant lands she had traveled to with her father, Captain Icterus, when she was an apprentice on *Oriole*—places like the sultanate of Callipepla, where the winds carry the perfume of a thousand spices, or the gray-towered city of Keastipol on the Great Southern Continent, where a dense and dangerous forest of giant trees along the coast dwindles away into a vast desert no one has ever mapped. If the crew heard Anna talking up there, apparently to herself or to Yah-Yah, they never let on or treated her as if they thought she was a bit funny in the head. Perhaps they never noticed; there's a lot to do to keep a ship sailing. At least the pirates were all quite happy to have Anna as captain, now that they knew she wasn't going to take *Shrike* away from them. And they all agreed that rescuing Captain Icterus and *Oriole*'s crew was a good reason to give up fishing.

Have you ever been to sea? I don't know how to describe it. The sails snapped as they caught the wind, the deck creaked, the ropes hummed, and the sound of the wind and the waves never stopped. The air was salt and clean and alive in a way it is no place on earth but over the ocean, and *Shrike* danced with the waves and the wind in a movement I still feel, when I close my eyes and listen to a storm in the pines.

Sometimes in the distance we would see herds of great whales, bigger—oh, you've never imagined anything like them, bigger than anything, bigger than a bear or a moose, as big as a dragon, but far more polite. They could have overturned the ship if they'd wanted, but they left us alone and we left them alone, although I talked to them, a little, at night. There were slim, sleek dolphins who scooted along with us, chattering like blue jays, certain life was one long joke. And there were many strange birds, ones that never come into the Wild Forest, things like albatrosses and puffins and storm-petrels. As we got into southern waters even the fish that slid away from *Shrike*'s racing shadow were different from the ones in the north, much more colorful, and some of them could fly.

Really and truly, I'm not making that up. These fish could

spread their fins out like wings, and when they leapt out of the water they could glide for quite a distance. Sometimes the unlucky ones would land on the deck; the pirates collected them and we had flying fish chowder.

Then one day the wind smelled different. It was heavy, wet instead of salt. Black clouds began to pile up, higher and higher, and as the sun rose they glowed a livid red along their edges.

"I don't like this," said Anna, and she had the lateen sail struck—that means they took it down.

I didn't like the weather either. The waves got higher and harder, and the ship rolled up green mountains and down into black valleys, rushing faster than she ever had yet. The wind slapped at the water, changing direction, now out of the northwest, now west, now south.

Anna ordered them to reef the mainsail, which means it was rolled up partway, so it wasn't so big. We raced on all day and into the night with just a little bit of sail to catch a little bit of wind so we could steer. A little bit of a storm is still a lot of wind, though, and oh, it was terrible.

It began to rain, great slashing sheets of rain, and the black sky burned white with lightning, and the thunder crashed like a mountain falling. And the waves—they were like mountains, as I said, mountains rearing over us, then breaking and falling, and every time I thought that was it, we would sink, we'd be dashed in pieces to the bottom of the sea by that stone-hard water. Then *Shrike* would come swooping up again, water rolling off her decks, and another wave would lift us up, up, up into the furious sky, and drop us sliding again down to where

there was nothing but water on all sides.

It was like a nightmare that went on and on and on, until it seemed there had never been anything but water, water in the sky, water on the decks, water leaking around the hatches into the hold, and pirates manning the pump that spat it out again. In the aftercastle all the biggest pirates were wrestling to hold the tiller steady, while the rest of us who weren't below pumping huddled in the forecastle out of the way, ready to dash out to the ropes if anything should come loose. All around us, poor *Shrike* creaked and groaned.

"It'll be all right," Anna told me, and she patted Yah-Yah reassuringly. "I've been through worse storms in *Oriole*, and *Oriole*'s smaller."

"She's just saying that to make you feel better," moaned Yah-Yah, cowering with her tail between her legs. "This is a really bad storm."

Then *Shrike* lurched and rolled in a new direction as the wind veered. We all fell in a heap, me and Anna and Yah-Yah and the pirates. From the aftercastle came a sudden chorus of shouting as the pirates there fought to keep the ship steady.

"I'd better go see how they're getting on back there," said Anna.

It's a captain's duty to keep her crew's spirits up, by letting them see that she isn't frightened and has confidence in them. That's what Anna was doing. She went out onto the deck, and the wind shrieked in through the open door.

Then the ship gave another lurch and roll, and the wind gusted around and hit us broadside on.

And Anna had just gone out on deck.

Yah-Yah and I thought the same thing at the same time, and we both flung ourselves out the door after her.

"Captain!" shouted Mirimick the bow master, and she came hurrying out, too, with the rest of the pirates who'd been in the forecastle behind her. There was water ankle-deep on the deck, pouring out through the scuppers back into the sea. A scupper, by the way, is a sort of hole in the side that lets water run off the deck.

But there was no Anna.

She must be in the aftercastle, I thought, but Yah-Yah barked and went skittering along the swaying, heaving deck, and I ran after her. *Shrike* heaved and bucked like she was trying to throw us off.

"Torrie!" cried Anna, and there she was, washed up against the rail and clinging on for dear life. But she wasn't crying for help, not she; she was captain of the ship and she had her crew to think of. She was crying a warning.

"Torrie, look out!"

Another wave struck, breaking over the starboard rail and lifting me off my feet. (Did I mention that starboard means the ship's right and port means the ship's left?) I went whirling away in the water, washing along the deck.

I heard Yah-Yah howl, and pirates shouting, "Hold on, Captain!" and then there was nothing but roaring water. I felt as though I were a stone in a landslide, bouncing down a hill. Except wetter. I tried to grab something, anything, and the wave tumbled me off smooth boards and snatched ropes from

my clutching fingers and toes. I stabbed with my spear and caught something and clung to it, while the wave ran on its way and left me battered and coughing, flat on the deck, clinging to my bronze-headed spear, which was driven into the boards.

After a while I sat up and rubbed salt water and fur out of my eyes. *Shrike* still pitched and tilted, but no more waves came over the side. Anna had caught Yah-Yah as the dog came tumbling down to the port rail, and the pirates had caught one another.

We all scrambled into the aftercastle, very wet and cold.

"Well, we probably needed a bath anyway," Anna said with a laugh, before going on to say encouraging things to the pirates, as though we all hadn't nearly gone into the sea.

After that last big wave the wind seemed to settle down and stick to one direction, and the waves were less exciting too. By afternoon of the next day we had only a light breeze to sail by, and the clouds were nothing but old dishcloths floating in a blue sky, above blue-green tropical waters.

But we had problems. Mirimick came and stood beside Anna and Mister Flytch, who were muttering and consulting tables of calculations and charts. They were trying to work out where we were, because we had been driven far off our course. The old lady pirate coughed, in that way that people do when they have to say something you won't want to hear.

"Captain Anna, sir," she said. "We have a little problem, dear."

"We won't be lost for long," said Anna grimly, busy with one of the brass devices that master mariners use for figuring out where they are, when they're far out at sea and there's nothing but the stars and the sun to steer by.

"It's not that, dear, sir," said Mirimick. "It's the water casks. Three of them got loose in the storm and went banging around and burst, and they banged and burst some of the others, too. We don't have enough drinking water left to get to the Granite Isles."

CHAPTER FOUR

In which we have no water

I think I was the only one who noticed how Anna's brown face paled and her lips tightened before she asked, "How much water do we have left?"

"Only two barrels, sir," said Mirimick.

"Two!" Mister Flytch exclaimed. "We'll have to turn back."

Anna shook her head and put a finger on the open chart before her. "We can't," she said.

"We can't go on," said the first mate. "It's foolishness."

"I'm not being foolish. Look again at where we are, Flytch."

Flytch looked where Anna pointed and he frowned. Then he used one of the brass devices to measure where the sun was in the sky, and then he looked at a book full of columns of numbers, and then he looked again at the chart—which is what sailors call a map. His frown deepened. He ran his finger along the little red ink spots where Anna had marked *Shrike*'s position every day. His whole body sagged, and he groaned.

"You're right, Captain," he said. "We can't turn back. We don't have enough water left to make it to land. Any land."

Yah-Yah lifted up her nose and howled.

"Hush," Anna said, dropping down on one knee to put her arms around the dog. "It's all right. We'll repair the water casks. Then when it rains, we can collect drinking water in them."

"That's right," said Mirimick. "I remember we were in trouble like this once before. We were in pursuit of a rich Callipeplan galley, and we'd come through a bit of a storm and lost nearly all our drinking water. Old Flytch was all for turning back …"

"No, I wasn't!" Flytch protested. "Not that time."

"But Captain Lanius said with a prize like that galley within reach he wasn't turning back for anything, and he had me stretch out the spare sail with a bit of a hole punched in it to funnel water into the casks so we'd be ready next time it rained, and on we went. We took that galley, too," Mirimick added dreamily. "It was loaded with silks and velvets and …"

"That was a long time ago," Mister Flytch said, with a guilty look at Anna.

"The point is …"

"The point is, we don't need to give up hope yet," Anna said.

But Yah-Yah was not comforted.

"We're going to die," she howled. "And then who will rescue Captain Icterus? Oow-oooooohhh!"

"We're not going to die," I said sternly. "Don't you trust Anna?"

Yah-Yah gave a faint, apologetic wag of her tail and licked Anna's face, but the truth was, the dog understood far better than I did just how much danger we were in.

We repaired the broken water casks and set a new course for the Granite Isles, hoping fervently for rain. We drank what water we had left very sparingly indeed. You have no idea how good old, swampy, warm water tastes, until you've drunk it knowing that there's hardly any left. Despite all our wishing, though, the sky went on being blue, and the sun went on being hot, so that I had to pour pails of seawater over Yah-Yah and myself to keep us cool.

Anna tried to pretend she wasn't afraid, to keep up the spirits of the crew, but I knew she was. I was afraid, too.

~~~~~

AT NIGHT, Anna tossed and turned in her hammock. Often she'd go out to pace back and forth on the deck, with Yah-Yah at her heels. Her face, at times like that, looked tight and old with worry, but whenever one of the crew went by, going to take their turn at the tiller, she merely looked thoughtful, staring up at the stars. But one night I saw in the moonlight how her face was shiny with tears, so I followed her and slipped my hand into hers.

"It'll be alright," I told her.

Anna shook her head. "We'll die," she said softly. "And my father will die, because no one will ever come to tell the pirate-queen where the treasure is and she'll never let him go. And the worst of it is, he'll never know what happened to me. He'll never know I tried to save him."

"He'll know," I said. It wasn't the most comforting thing to say, but she squeezed my hand anyway, as though I'd helped. Maybe she knew I needed comforting, too.

I WAS UP ON TOP OF THE FORECASTLE THE NEXT DAY, looking down at the undrinkable salt water bubbling and rolling below, when Anna came to join me. We had only a pailful of water left in the last barrel, and everyone was tired and glum, everyone was hot and parched. Our lips were cracked, our tongues stiff and swollen. We couldn't survive more than another day or two, and we all knew it.

Anna sat beside me, dangling her bare feet down and biting the end of her pigtail.

"I'm sorry about last night, Torrie," she said awkwardly. "About crying, I mean. I didn't mean to."

"Everybody needs to cry sometimes," I said. "Even heroes."

She scowled. "I'm not a hero," she said. "I'm a useless captain. I'm sorry I got you to come with me," she added, before I could ask why she thought she was useless. "You belong in the Wild Forest, and you're going to die out here on the empty sea."

I shrugged. "You didn't 'get' me to come. I made you let me join you. And no one ever said adventures were safe."

"The crew isn't blaming me. I don't know why. They should."

"For what?"

"I'm the captain. I'm supposed to be responsible."

"For what?"

"For everything."

"How can you be?" I asked practically. "If you were responsible for everything, you wouldn't need a crew to sail the ship, you could do it yourself."

She wasn't really listening to me. "I nearly lost the ship in the storm. We've come a long distance out of our way, and now we have no water."

"Nonsense," I told her, sounding far more cheerful than I felt. "You couldn't help the storm, Anna. That wasn't your fault. You brought us through it just fine. You've figured out where we are. You know which direction we need to go to get to the Granite Isles. The water casks breaking free and smashing up was bad luck. And it still might rain."

But the sun was glaring, yellow-white in an unclouded sky.

Anna just sighed.

"I should have made certain there were new ropes holding those casks in place instead of weak old ones. I never thought of it, but I should have. I'm the *captain*. The ship is my responsibility."

"You can't undo it now," I said.

Anna nodded grimly. "Exactly. I can't. And I can't do anything to make things better."

I thought this was likely to be true. I couldn't do anything to make things better either, and that made me sigh as well. In all my adventures, I don't think I'd ever felt quite so hopeless. A lack of water wasn't something you could go out and fight, telling yourself that even a faint hope of winning was better than none. Thirst was something that would always win in the end.

"I'm sure we'll manage," I said. "It's bound to rain soon."

And I lay on my back and stared up into the burning sky, looking for a cloud, for even the faintest smudge of haze, that might mean the weather would change.

The sky was blue, blue and blue and blue forever. I peered around at the circle of horizon and it was the same. The only thing that interrupted the blueness was a speckling of black—it was birds, far away. I watched them, because we hadn't seen any birds since the storm and they were something different to look at from the unbroken sky.

And then I thought about what birds might mean.

"Anna!" I said, jumping up. "Look!"

She looked where I pointed.

"I don't see anything," she said.

"Birds!"

Anna frowned. She shaded her eyes with her hands and stared for a long time. Then she shook her head.

"I can't see a thing. Wait here. Don't lose sight of them."

She went down the ladder, back to her tiny cabin in the aftercastle, and returned with her telescope.

"Show me where to look, Torrie," she said, so I pointed with my spear and she sighted along it.

"Birds!" she said. "Terns, I think. Good work, Torrie!" And she hugged me, before she went leaping back down the ladder again.

"Change course!" she shouted. "South by southeast, Mister Flytch! Torrie's spotted a flock of fishing terns, and at this time of year they'll be feeding nestlings. We can make land!"

The pirates all stared at her.

"It's the sun," said Mirimick at last. "Poor dear. You'd better come lie down, Captain."

"What? No!" said Anna. "This is no time to lie down!"

"*Who* did you say had sighted terns?" asked Mister Flytch.

"Torrie!" said Anna. "My friend Torrie. Er ... he's invisible."

"Ah," said Mister Flytch, and Mirimick shook her head sadly.

Anna stamped her foot. "Don't you look at me like that. I'm your captain. Torrie, you'd better let them see you."

So I did.

"A goblin!" shouted Mirimick.

Mister Flytch grabbed Anna and jerked her away. "Look out, Captain!" he said. "It'll bite you!"

"That's Torrie," said Anna. "He's not a goblin." And as I

opened my mouth she added, "And he's not a brownie, either."

"What is he, then?" asked Mirimick suspiciously.

"I'm Torrie," I said, with great dignity. "The oldest of the Old Things of the Wild Forest. But that doesn't matter right now. What matters is finding land."

"And water," said Yah-Yah. "Finding water matters. The terns could be nesting on nothing more than a lump of rock."

"You really like to look on the bright side, don't you, Yah-Yah," I said.

Still giving me suspicious looks, as if he thought I might suddenly start drooling and snapping like a mad dog, Mister Flytch brought out the charts and checked them.

"There's no land marked anywhere in this region," he said. "Could be you've discovered an unknown island, Captain."

"If it is an island," said Anna, less happily. "It could be just a lump of rock."

"See?" said Yah-Yah to me.

"But it's the best hope we've got. Alter course, Mister Flytch."

"Aye aye, sir!" said Mister Flytch. "Gladly! All hands who don't have something better to do, keep a lookout! We don't want to miss it."

Anna climbed up the mast with her telescope to watch for the first sign of the island. I joined her and we both searched the horizon eagerly.

For the longest time there was nothing to be seen. Even my birds disappeared. I began to be afraid I had imagined them. Then, so far away that at first I didn't really notice, there was a dim, grayish smudge on the horizon.

"Anna?" I whispered, and pointed. "Look there."

I didn't want to get the hopes of the crew up, if I was just imagining the smudge. After all, it was very hot, and I was very furry. Maybe my head had gotten too hot and I was going mad. It can happen to you in the tropics.

Anna trained the telescope on the smudge and she began to grin.

"It's green," she said. "Trees. That means water. You've saved us, Torrie."

"Whoo-heee!" I whooped. Anna yelped and covered her ears with her arms, hanging on to the yard, which is the crosspiece the sail hangs from, with just her leg hooked over it.

"Don't yell in my ears!" she said. "Anyway, 'Whoo–heee' isn't the proper thing to say. You say, 'Land ho.' But shout down at the deck, all right?"

I cupped my hands around my mouth. "Land–hoooo!" I bellowed.

Anna shinnied back down the mast and I slid to the deck after her.

"Land, land, land!" I sang, dancing around Yah-Yah, and the dog spun in a circle chasing her tail, barking.

"You should sing, 'Water, water, water,'" said Mister Flytch. "That's the important thing." He offered me his big callused hand to shake, and Mirimick patted me cautiously on the head.

"It's alright," I told the bow master. "I hardly ever bite."

"We'll add the island to the charts," said Anna. "Torrie Island, it'll be."

Torrie Island. That still makes me feel like one of the great explorers, having an island named after me. But of course it was Anna's navigation and all her calculations with her brass devices that really put it on the map. It was just luck, and the fact that I have much better eyesight than humans, that I discovered it. Still, it was me. Even if someone else was there first …

CHAPTER FIVE

In which Anna takes a prisoner

orrie Island was small. It wasn't surprising that other explorers had missed it. But it was green and alive, and that was all we cared about. Such a place was bound to have fresh water; at the very least there would be rain-filled pools.

That evening we swung at anchor in a little bay. Along the shore, trees with huge, long leaves, leaves like ferns and grass and dragonfly wings, whispered together in the least little breeze. Anna ordered the boat lowered and a few of us went ashore on a quick scouting expedition. We found where a stream spread out slick and shining over the white sand, and rowed up it until it grew narrow, twisting between moist black banks overhung with creeping vines. There, above the reach of the tide, the water was fresh. It tasted almost sweet, after the sour, stale sludge that was all we had left on *Shrike*.

We filled one of the big water casks; tomorrow we could

replenish the rest. For now, Anna and the pirates just piled the boat with bananas and coconuts, and on the way back, we caught a basket full of crabs on the beach, to make a change from salt beef and fish.

Early the next morning we started to fill the rest of our repaired water casks. They could only fit one at a time in the boat, and it took almost the whole crew, turning the capstan that wound up the rope on the little wooden crane, to heave them aboard *Shrike*. I was on the ship, singing to the pirates as they pushed the capstan's bars to raise the second-last barrel, and the very last filled water cask was being rowed back to *Shrike* by Anna and Mister Flytch, when I saw something alarming.

"Avast!" I shouted. "Ahoy!" Neither of those seemed quite the right thing to say. "Look out! There's someone on the beach!"

The pirates didn't stop turning the capstan, but Mirimick dashed into the forecastle and came out again with her crossbow, cranking the windlass that wound it up for shooting. From the top of the forecastle she watched the man on the beach. Anna and Flytch were rowing twice as fast now. You never knew with people on islands. They could be anybody.

This man didn't look very dangerous. He was wearing ragged old trousers and a ragged old shirt and a really terrible hat made out of banana leaves, and he was jumping around like there were crabs pinching his toes.

"Hey, hey, hey!" he was shouting. "Come back, come back!"

Mirimick and I kept watch while the boat came alongside and the pirates lifted the last cask aboard.

"Are there any others hiding in the jungle?" Anna called up, and Mirimick scanned the shore with Anna's telescope.

"No, sir," she shouted down. "Just him."

"All right, then, we'll go back," said Anna. "Keep a good lookout. It might be a trick."

"Wait for me," I said, scrambling down into the boat with Anna and the first mate. My spear and I were probably better guards than a bunch of old pirates.

The man on the shore, though, seemed to be afraid that *Shrike* was about to swing the boat aboard and leave without him. Yelling, "Wait, wait, oh, please wait!" he dashed out into the clear blue-green waters of the bay, tripping and stumbling, and finally he swam, still shouting, "Oh, please wait!" He swallowed lots of water, because you shouldn't swim and shout at the same time.

"Man the tiller, Torrie," said Anna. "Keep her steady." She and Flytch leaned into their oars, dip, swish, out, dip, swish, out, and the boat cut through the water like an arrow.

The young man was treading water when we got to him. I grabbed him by his hair, which was long and blond and tangled, and then Mister Flytch and Anna heaved him into the boat over the stern. He lay on the bottom of the boat with a big pool of water running off him, while we turned around to head for *Shrike*.

"Rescue," the man said, when he had coughed out enough water to be able to sit up. "Rescue at last. Thank you, thank you, thank you."

"What happened to you?" asked Anna.

"How long have you been there?" asked Flytch.

"You haven't given the island a name, have you?" I asked. "Because it's Torrie Island now."

The man looked at me and rubbed his eyes.

"What's that?" he asked.

"That's my friend Torrie," said Anna. "He discovered the island."

"You can call the island whatever you want," he said, still staring at me. "Just get me off it. Take me home!"

"But how did you get there?" asked Anna. "Did your ship

sink? And how long have you been there?" She wrinkled her nose up at his clothes, which, although well-washed, were really just rags.

The man shuddered. "I was swept overboard in a hurricane," he said. "It must be …" he paused and counted on his fingers, "over two years I've been on this wretched island with nothing but crabs and bananas and coconuts to eat—not that I'm complaining about that, it's better than seaweed. But please, will your captain take me home, do you think?"

"My island is not wretched," I said.

"We'll leave you at the first convenient port," said Anna.

"Please," said the man. "Let me talk to your captain. I need to go straight home. You'll be greatly rewarded. My mother— I'm her only son. She must believe I'm dead. She'll be so grateful to have me back. You won't lose anything by going out of your way. I swear it."

"We're in a hurry," said Anna. "You're a sailor. You'll be able to work your way home from any port."

"My mother is Queen Nevilla of the Granite Isles," said the young man. "Your captain will understand why he should take me straight home."

Anna and Mister Flytch and I all looked at one another.

"Ah," said Anna. "I see. So if we take you straight home to the Granite Isles, the queen will give us a rich reward?"

"Exactly."

"And if we leave you at some port to work your way home while we go about our respectable merchant's business, the pirate-queen will be very annoyed with us when you do get home, and she might send ships to find us, to tell us how annoyed she is?"

The young man looked embarrassed. "Well," he said. "Um, yes. I don't like making threats, but you see, I am her only child, and you have to imagine how she must feel, believing me dead. I want to get home and set her mind at ease as soon as possible."

"Hmm," said Anna, and she grinned at me and Flytch. It was the sort of grin I expect her grandfather Lanius the pirate, the terror of the seas, must have grinned when he saw a big fat merchant vessel waddling over the waves.

"Lucky for you, then, that I'm the captain of this ship, and we're not respectable merchants," said Anna. "Nothing would make me happier than taking you straight home to the Granite Isles, Your Highness." And her grin grew broader, as the boat came alongside *Shrike* without a bump and the waiting crew dropped a rope to us. "It just so happens that the Granite Isles are our destination. Welcome aboard the *Shrike*. I'm Captain Anna. Granddaughter of Captain Lanius. I expect you've heard of him."

For a moment I don't think the prince understood what Anna had said. He was staring at her with a sort of astonished look in his brown eyes. Then I poked him with my spear to make him climb the rope up *Shrike*'s side. He blinked like he was just waking up, and began to climb.

"But Captain Lanius the pirate has been dead for years," said the prince, when we were all aboard *Shrike* again.

"True," said Anna. "Nevertheless, this is the *Shrike*, and you're my prisoner."

"Captain …" the man protested. "You can't rescue someone and then take him prisoner."

"Tell your mother that," snapped Anna, and her blue and green eyes both blazed. Her hand was on the hilt of her sword.

Mister Flytch dropped his enormous hand on the pirate-prince's shoulder and pulled him away to safety. "This way, Your Highness," he said. "We'd better get you dried off."

"Come on, Anna," I said, tugging at her shirt. "If you throw him overboard again, you won't be able to make a deal with his mother."

Anna let me lead her off to the top of the forecastle. She was so angry she was trembling all over.

"How dare he!" she said, through clenched teeth. "Saying we can't rescue him and take him prisoner, when his own mother did the exact same thing to my father when *Oriole* had to put in to the Granite Isles for shelter!"

"If he's been on my island for two years, he wouldn't know about that," I said. "You can't blame him for what his mother did."

"I suppose so," said Anna grudgingly.

"This makes everything a lot simpler," said Yah-Yah. "We just trade this prince for Captain Icterus and his crew. No foolish treasure-hunting or dangerous jail-breaking."

"What if his mother doesn't want him back?" I asked.

"Of course she will," said Yah-Yah.

"Well, she's a pirate. Maybe he's lying and she marooned him on the island herself. I'd better ask him."

"What's Yah-Yah saying?" Anna asked. "Torrie, what are you going to ask the prince? Come back here!"

She ran after me as I scampered down into the forecastle.

The prince was wearing Mirimick's spare shirt and trousers. With his long hair tied into a nautical pigtail and his little beard neatly combed, he looked quite respectable, although not very grand or royal, because Mirimick's spare clothes left lots of his wrists and ankles bare. Probably the clothes of one of the men would have fitted him better, but Mirimick was the only one of the old pirates who had done any laundry lately. Nobody really likes washing clothes in salt water; it makes them all stiff and scratchy. But some people think stiff and scratchy is better than sweaty and smelly. Only some people, unfortunately.

"Are you sure your mother will want you back, Your Highness?" I asked. "It wasn't her who left you on the island in the first place?"

That seemed to me the sort of thing a pirate-queen might do, although to tell the truth I'd never heard of Queen Nevilla marooning people, or even making very many people walk the plank. Prisoners, in her opinion, seemed to be much more valuable alive.

"Her who marooned me? No!" The pirate-prince stared at me in horror. "It was not! My mother isn't a cruel woman."

"Maybe you don't know her all that well," snapped Anna.

"What do you mean by that?" demanded the prince. "What do you know about it?"

Mister Flytch poked him with a big knobbly forefinger. "Captain," he prompted the prince.

"What do you know about it, Captain?" muttered the prisoner.

"More than you, apparently," said Anna.

"Hah!" said the prince, which didn't seem to me at all the sort of thing he ought to say right now.

Anna ground her teeth.

"Bow master!" she ordered Mirimick. "Take the prisoner below and tie him up where he can't do any damage."

"Aye aye, Captain," said Mirimick. "Come along, dear," she added to the prince.

Anna scowled as the prisoner was led past her, and the young man shied away from her. I would have, too. Her eyes glittered and her hair sprang out of its braid and nearly crackled, and her fingers kept clenching and unclenching on the hilt of her sword. I imagine her grandfather Lanius looked a lot like that when he was thinking about making someone walk the plank.

There was a shout and a thump from the deck. We all ran out. I was there first, just in time to see that Mirimick had fallen sprawling. The prince leapt to the rail, about to hurl himself overboard again. Obviously he'd decided Torrie Island, with its fresh water and plentiful food and shady trees, was nicer than being a prisoner tied up in a pirate's hold.

I flung myself after the prince, caught him around the ankles, and jerked him back. We both went crashing to the deck, rolling over and over into a coil of rope. Everyone else came running to untangle us and help Mirimick up.

"I'm getting too old for this," the bow master groaned, rubbing her bruised hip.

"Remember, you're only as old as you feel, Mirimick," said

the first mate, as he tried to grab the prisoner by his shirt collar. He missed, and Mirimick sniggered.

"Feeling old and slow?" she asked, as Flytch snatched again.

"Help me!" whispered the prince in my ear, squirming and thrashing away from Mister Flytch. "You're not a pirate. You seem like an honorable creature. Help me!"

And then Anna was there, resting the point of her sword on the pirate-prince's chest.

"All right," she said grimly. "Get up and hold out your hands."

The prince's hands were roped together and he was sent down into the hold, where he was tied to a ring in the wall.

Mirimick was still limping a little when she and I took him down a blanket and a bowl of fish chowder, which she fed him with a big wooden spoon.

"Sorry," the prince said, looking a bit ashamed of himself when he saw who had brought him his meal. "Did I hurt you?"

"Don't worry about it, dear," Mirimick said. "In your place I'd have done the same thing."

"Really?" he asked, looking a bit doubtful. She did look a lot like a sweet old lady, except for the long knife stuck in her boot.

"Well, of course, dear. It's a prisoner's duty to try to escape. But you really should have pulled me over the side with you, instead of knocking me down on the deck. If we were both in the water, the captain would have wanted to rescue me first, and you might have gotten away. You have to plan these things, you know." She winked. "Of course, we'd have just sent Torrie and his spear to fetch you back again."

The prince gave her a worried smile. I could see he wasn't sure if she was teasing him or not. He went on eating his chowder in silence, while Mirimick fed him like an overgrown baby, even wiping his chin with her sleeve when the wooden spoon dribbled some. He kept trying to catch my attention every time the bow master glanced away, grimacing at me and waggling his eyebrows in a significant manner. But I couldn't bring myself to meet his gaze.

CHAPTER SIX

In which we change our plans

The next few days of our voyage weren't pleasant at all. Anna went around scowling, so that the old pirates were very quiet and careful to keep out of her way, and the pirate-prince, whose name was Frederik, sat around looking morose and dejected. At least Anna had let him out of the hold, once we were far enough from Torrie Island that there was no fear of him swimming back.

I spent most of my time sitting right out at the tip of the bowsprit, with all *Shrike* behind me and nothing but air and foaming water on all sides. The bowsprit, by the way, is the spar or pole that sticks out of the front of the ship, with ropes and things fastened to it to help hold up the mast.

Finally, though, I had to talk to Frederik again, to explain why I wasn't going to help him. I'd been avoiding him when I could, because he kept trying to catch my eye, and I was starting to feel guilty. He seemed like the sort of prince I was usually quite happy to rescue.

I walked up to where he was sitting, and I felt just awful. My stomach ached, as if I'd eaten a turtle, shell and all. Just a big hard lump.

"I'm sorry," I said. "I can't help you. It wouldn't be right. I'm Anna's friend, and you're her prisoner."

And I walked away again.

"Torrie!" he called after me. "Torrie!"

I ignored him and climbed back onto the bowsprit.

Frederik followed me. I'd forgotten that as well as being a prisoner he was a sailor, and could climb along the bowsprit almost as easily as I could.

"Torrie!" he said, sitting astride the bowsprit, which was bucking like an angry horse as the ship ran up and down the waves. "At least tell me why! Why am I a prisoner? Why does the captain hate me so much? What did I ever do to her? I don't hate her, even though it was her grandfather Lanius who ruined the Granite Isles."

"What?" I asked. "Anna didn't tell me that."

"She wouldn't, would she? She's his granddaughter." But then he added, more fairly, "She probably doesn't know."

"What did he do?"

"First, tell me why Anna's so angry at me."

"It's her father," I said. "Your mother has her father, Captain Icterus, a prisoner in her dungeon."

"Oh," said Frederik. "Why? I mean, yes, I know my mother keeps prisoners in her dungeon quite often." He looked a little guilty, admitting that. "But not sea captains. Just wealthy people, nobles and great lords she can get ransoms for."

"Anna says it's because of a treasure her grandfather hid somewhere. The pirate-queen wants it, and she's holding Captain Icterus prisoner until he tells her where it is. Except Icterus doesn't know and Anna does."

"Why doesn't Anna just tell my mother? Then her father will be set free and everyone will be happy."

"Anna was going to find the treasure herself and then make the queen release Captain Icterus," I said. "But now that she has you she doesn't need to. The queen would probably do anything to get you back."

"But the treasure …" said Frederik.

"Treasure, treasure, treasure," I said, and I was quite angry. "What is it with you pirates and treasure? Treasure's fun, fine. I've gone searching for a few treasures in my time, and found them, too. But the fun is in finding them, not having them. It's just treasure; it doesn't matter, not compared to someone's freedom. All you pirates are the same!"

"But Torrie," Frederik protested. "This treasure …"

"Go away," I said. I couldn't go away myself, as he was between me and the ship. "I don't want to talk to you anymore."

"But Torrie …" he said again.

"Go away," I said. I bared my teeth at him, and I know my eyes gleamed, very wild and dangerous. I am. People forget that sometimes. Frederik went away.

"Torrie!"

"I said …" I began to say, but this voice was Yah-Yah's. I

turned around and went back along the bowsprit to the fore-castle. It was sort of like walking along a thin willow bough in a hurricane. And I wasn't using my hands, either. Just you try it sometime, if you think it sounds easy.

"Did you hear what that pirate said?" I demanded. "He's a prisoner, and he knows Anna's father is a prisoner, and still all he can think about is the treasure."

"He can't help being a pirate," said Yah-Yah.

"Can't help!" I exclaimed. "I thought you hated pirates."

Yah-Yah folded her ears back apologetically. "I think he's sort of sweet," she said.

"Phah!"

I'd thought this was going to be a nice adventure—we'd find the treasure, which would be fun, and then we'd trade the treasure for Anna's father, which would make Anna and her father both happy. It wasn't turning out that way at all. Anna would still get her father back, but she was mad at Frederik just for being the pirate-queen's son, and despite the fact that I had at first thought he seemed a decent sort, he was turning out to be just a greedy, treasure-hungry pirate like his mother. And Yah-Yah, the pirate-hater who should have been the one creature on my side in not liking Frederik, *Yah-Yah* thought he was *sweet*.

"What do you want?" I snarled at Yah-Yah.

Yah-Yah growled back, and I have to admit she had a much nastier growl than I do. "What are you in such a bad mood for?" she asked. "*Your* father's not in a dungeon. I came to ask you to talk to Anna. Cheer her up."

"Why does she need cheering up?" I asked. "She has Frederik as a hostage. She'll have her father back soon."

"I don't know why she's so glum," said Yah-Yah patiently. "That's why I want you to talk to her."

It was hard to say no to Yah-Yah when she looked at me so beseechingly, with her head tilted to one side and her ears folded back.

"All right," I grumped. Yah-Yah wagged her tail and tried to lick me, happy now that she'd got me to do what she wanted. I dodged her slobbering tongue. I wasn't in a mood for drool.

I found Anna in the aftercastle, looking at charts and biting her braid.

"Hi!" I said, climbing up on her, piggyback, so I could look over her shoulder. "I'm supposed to cheer you up."

"I'm busy," Anna said. "Do you have to do that? You're tickling my ear, and you're heavy."

"No, I'm not," I said. "And I can see you're terribly, terribly busy. You're looking at the same charts you were looking at last night. Let's play a game." I jumped down onto the table and sat there on the chart, so she couldn't ignore me.

"What kind of game?" asked Anna.

"Umm…" I said. "I'll tell you why I don't like Frederik, and then you have to tell me why you don't like him."

"That's not a game," said Anna.

"Yes, it is," I said. "It's called, 'Why I Don't Like Frederik.' Come on, it's lots of fun."

Anna tried to scowl, but she ended up smiling instead.

"Silly," she said. "All right. But I thought you liked him. Everybody else does."

"Even Yah-Yah likes him," I agreed. "So why don't you?"

"You said you were going to go first," Anna pointed out.

"Oh," I said. "Well, I don't like him because he's just a boring pirate and once you mention treasure that's all he can think about. I expected better of him." And I folded my arms over my chest. "So there."

Anna actually laughed. "My turn, then. I don't like him because he's the pirate-queen's son." Then she made a face. "Actually, trying not to like him … I guess that's been making me angry at myself more than at him, because I know I'm not being fair when I blame him for what his mother did. He's not as bad as you say," she added. "He's never mentioned treasure to me once."

"I didn't think you talked to him."

She shrugged. "I have, a little. We played cribbage while you and Yah-Yah were hunting rats in the hold last night."

"Oh," I said. I patted my spear. "We killed a whole dozen. I thought rat chowder would make a nice change, but Mister Flytch said he'd throw me overboard if he caught me anywhere near the chowder pot with a rat, so Yah-Yah and I roasted them and ate them all ourselves. Mirimick thought they smelled good, until she saw what they were." I could tell from Anna's grimace that she didn't even want to think about roasted rat, so I quickly asked, "What did you and Frederik talk about?"

"Just things. Places we'd sailed to. If he was just some sailor, not the pirate-queen's son, I think we'd probably be friends. You know, he's not much older than me, and he wasn't just a captain. He was in charge of a whole fleet of his mother's war galleys. Admiral of a whole fleet." She sounded rather admiring of this achievement, and a bit envious, too.

"A whole *pirate* fleet," I said scornfully. "I suppose he's seized the cargoes of scores of ships and taken dozens of wealthy hostages himself. He's probably just as bad as his mother."

Anna shrugged, which I took to mean that he probably had and that she didn't want to talk about it. That worried me.

"You're not getting pirate ideas yourself, are you?" I asked.

Anna changed the topic, or at least, she went back to what we had originally been talking about. "Frederik never mentioned treasure at all," she said again. "In fact, I never mentioned treasure to him … Torrie! You didn't go and tell him about my grandfather's treasure?"

"Well," I muttered guiltily. "I might have. Just, you know, explaining why your father was a prisoner in the first place."

"Torrie!"

"It was an accident. And anyway, what harm can it do?"

"Er…" said a voice from the doorway. "Am I interrupting?"

It was Frederik.

"Yes," said Anna. "You are."

"Oh, good," he said, and he came on in. "I was wondering if I could talk to you, Captain."

"No," said Anna.

"About the treasure."

"Absolutely not," said Anna.

"Because you see, I don't think you understand about it."

"We understand everything we need to," I said, with great dignity.

"No, you don't," said Frederik. "I don't think you do at all. It explains everything."

"We don't want to listen," said Anna.

"How does it explain everything?" I asked. I'm curious, I know. I can't help it. It's why I end up on so many adventures. Most Old Things have better sense than to go off adventuring; they just stay safely home in the Wild Forest, where the only dangers are things like goblins and enchanters and curses and dragons. No sense of adventure or curiosity about the wider world at all, most of them.

"Torrie!" said Anna. "We don't care if he can explain anything!"

"Well, maybe we do," I said. "That old saying, 'Curiosity killed the cat,' is a lie, you know. I've met that cat myself, and she told me what really happened was ..."

"What cat? Torrie, we don't care about any cat, we're talking about ..."

"*Anyhow,*" said Frederik loudly, "this treasure, it must be the thing that your grandfather stole from the Granite Isles. It's no wonder my mother would do anything to get it back. Have you ever been to the Granite Isles, either of you?"

"No," I said.

"Of course not," said Anna.

"Well, they're very bleak, and barren, and nothing grows. If you plant a tree, it grows for a year or two and then it withers up. If you plant a potato, it grows a few little potatoes the size of marbles, and the squash are no bigger than mangoes, and the few old mango trees that still survive never have more than one or two fruit. The goats are thin and give hardly any milk, because there's not much that grows for even a goat to eat. Even the fish in the rivers and bays are small and bony. We eat seaweed, when we haven't managed to seize enough gold from passing ships to buy rice and potatoes."

"It sounds awful," I said.

"It *is* awful. And my mother has always said that it's all Captain Lanius's fault."

I didn't believe that. It couldn't be true. It would take a very, very powerful enchanter to put a curse on a whole kingdom. It wasn't the sort of thing a pirate could do.

"My grandfather was a pirate, but he wasn't a sorcerer," said Anna. "He wouldn't have known how to put a curse on a place."

"Exactly what I was thinking," I said.

"He didn't have to be a sorcerer," said Frederik. "He probably never even realized what he'd done. *Shrike* used to sail to the Granite Isles, back when my mother was a young girl-queen. Mirimick told me how beautiful the islands were then. She said they were such a nice peaceful *green* place to drop anchor and have a rest, and that there used to be such nice dances at the palace, before Lanius decided to raid it. I can't image Lanius's pirates ever being invited to dances at the palace, but there you are. Isn't it obvious?"

"Um," I said. "No."

"My mother's always said Lanius caused the curse that blighted the islands. So whatever it was he stole, taking it away caused the curse. If my mother could get it back, the Isles would be green and fertile again. We wouldn't have to be pirates."

"Hah! That's what you say now," said Anna. "Once a pirate, always a pirate."

"We Granite Islanders never wanted to be pirates," said Frederik. "Even my mother—I know everyone calls her the pirate-queen, but she's a queen first, you know, and a pirate only because she has to be, to survive."

"She's awfully good at it," said Anna angrily.

"You should talk," said Frederik. "Your grandfather, he was a pirate because he wanted to be, because it was easier than honest work. No, I'm sorry, I shouldn't have said that," he added, as Anna's eyes snapped and she opened her mouth to retort. "Your grandfather's not your fault. Just listen, Anna! Do you know what I really want to do? I want to grow things. I want to plant trees!"

"So go plant trees and leave honest merchants alone," Anna muttered.

"I get smugglers to bring me trees from the mainland," said Frederik, dreamily. "Pines and mangoes and lemons, cinnamon and nutmeg and camphor. I plant them on the cool mountains and in the hot valleys. I dig irrigation ditches and I mulch them with seaweed—and they always die. Things just can't grow on the Granite Isles anymore. You know, we used to have forests? I want to plant a forest."

"Why don't you all emigrate to someplace you could live more happily, then?" Anna demanded.

"A lot of people have left," said Frederik. "But you see, the

Isles are our *home*. And for some people home just isn't a place you can leave. It gets into your blood and you love it, no matter how desolate and hard a place it is."

"Like the sea," Anna said.

Frederik nodded. "Exactly like that. A place you can't get out of your heart. When I'm sailing home and get my first sight of the three islands, catching the last rays of the sun so that they look like gold and rubies—I'm never happier. The sound of the brooks and waterfalls in the mountains of the interior is like music, ringing from valley to valley, and when you stand on the beaches and look at the curving lowland hills against the sky, you know there's no more beautiful land." Then he sighed. "But the mountains used to be covered in forests and terraces where we grew potatoes and grapes, and the hills had green fields and orchards and forests and gardens of flowers. I've seen paintings of them."

"And you think it's all my grandfather's fault?" Anna asked.

"I told you," said Frederik. "Captain Lanius stole something, and the curse came."

"You don't know that's the reason."

"I'm pretty sure. My mother is convinced of it."

"What exactly was the treasure, then?"

"I don't know," said Frederik. "She's never told me. I think maybe it's some sort of royal secret. She probably thought I wasn't responsible enough yet to know."

"It sounds pretty fishy to me," said Anna. "I don't think something like that is possible."

"Well," I said, "I've heard of magical things working like that."

They both looked at me. "Like how?" Anna asked.

"By holding all the goodness of the land. A magic thing like that is the sort of thing a really powerful enchanter might make, if, say, he or she wanted to go off and found a colony someplace where the land was no good."

It all sounded very familiar, actually. I'd heard a story long, long ago, about an enchanter-king, whose brother drove him from his kingdom. He sailed away with his loyal followers and his little daughter and landed on some distant, desert island, which he turned into a paradise with his magic. A distant, desert island, I wondered, or three bare, rocky islands in the South Seas?

"Your first king wasn't an enchanter, was he?" I asked.

Frederik shrugged and turned a little red with embarrassment. "I didn't pay much attention to my history tutor, I'm afraid. I was more interested in natural history. I used to run off to the mountains …"

"Well, it sounds to me as if this treasure was something made to make the land fertile," I interrupted, before Frederik could get all wistful and dreamy about his trees again. "I'm sure of it. And when a thing like that is taken away, everything good and growing fails. I've heard stories."

"Stories." Anna raised one eyebrow and looked very skeptical.

"Dragons are stories," I told her sternly. "And I've fought one. So don't say 'stories' in that tone of voice. There's all sorts of truth in stories."

"I'd have thought that … whatever Torrie is, was a story," said Frederik helpfully. "And then I met him."

"But what about my father?" said Anna, and for a moment I thought her voice was trembling. I patted her hand.

"My mother's dungeon isn't that bad," said the prince. "It's nice and cool and airy. I used to play down there in the summer, when I was a boy. And Mum never feeds her prisoners any worse than anyone else on the island is eating. I mean, it might be seaweed soup and boiled rice, but only if everyone else, even in the palace, is eating seaweed soup and boiled rice. Sometimes that's all we can get, if we haven't gotten any big ransoms lately, or taken any good cargoes."

"It's still a dungeon," Anna said angrily, pushing her chair back from the table. "And if your mother has hurt my father, I'm going to attack her palace myself, and I'll do worse than my grandfather did. He just stole things. I'll make sure there's not a wall left standing."

"I'm certain Captain Icterus is fine," Frederik reassured her. "I mean, he must be unhappy, but Anna, surely it wouldn't take you much longer to find the treasure than it would just to take me home and negotiate with my mother, would it? I need to find this treasure, if you really know where it is. Besides, just think, if you have me and the treasure both to bargain with, Mum's going to give you anything you want, you can count on it."

"I don't want anything," said Anna. "Just my father and his crew and his ship."

I didn't really understand Frederik then, and even though I'd figured out what sort of powers the treasure must have, I still didn't really understand what it meant. I still thought Frederik's eagerness to go treasure-hunting a bit odd. After all, he had been cast away on an island for two years. His mother no doubt thought he was dead. He should be so eager to get home that not all the treasure on earth would slow him down. He should have been insisting that we take him straight to the Granite Isles and trade him for Anna's father and his crew.

I pointed this out.

"Tomorrow or next month, my mother will be just as happy when I turn up alive," said Frederik. "I know you think I'm a treasure-obsessed pirate, Torrie. But I'm not. I'm a prince. Don't you understand that yet? I have a duty to do what's best for my people. And if I'm right—if *you're* right—about this treasure, then finding it would make life for all of us in the Isles so much better. There would be fish in the bays and grain in the fields, plenty of food ... try to imagine what that would mean for the Granite Isles! No more piracy, no more holding people for ransom! I can put off going home for a short while, to make that possible. I have to, no matter how badly I want to see my mother again. It's my duty. And she'd say the same thing."

Princes and princesses, kings and queens, had to think of the good of their people—I did understand that. He wasn't the first prince I'd known. I just hadn't realized that he really was more a prince than a pirate.

"I know I don't seem very royal," Frederik said, as if *he* had to apologize.

"You seemed very royal just then," I said humbly. "I'm sorry for doubting you. I was thinking of you as just another pirate. Of course you're right, and we should find the treasure, if there's a chance it can save the Granite Isles."

Anna had been listening to everything Frederik said, chewing on the end of her braid and frowning a little, the way she did when she was deep in thought. But she didn't look angry anymore. After a moment she sighed and held out a hand to Frederik.

"I'm sorry, too," she said. "Torrie's right. If we can change things for the Granite Isles, and stop them preying on other people's shipping, we should. And it won't take us much longer than going straight to see your mother."

Frederik and Anna shook hands solemnly, as if they'd just met for the first time.

I jumped to my feet, so we could see the charts I'd been sitting on. "Where do we start?" I asked. "How close are we? Will we need spades? You can't hunt treasure without a spade."

Anna straightened the top chart, the one she had been frowning over when I first came in.

"There," she said, pointing. "That island."

"It looks like a little speck," I said. "It can't be a very big treasure."

"That?" said Prince Frederik. "Serpent Island? I used to go fishing in the waters off there. It's the nearest place to the Granite Isles where there are decent-sized fish. The treasure's been that close to home all these years?"

"Don't get any ideas," said Anna. "You'll never find it by yourself."

"Captain," said Frederik, looking hurt. "I give you my word, I wouldn't double-cross you, no matter what was at stake."

"Huh," Anna grunted, and looked a little ashamed of herself. "Sorry," she said. "So, you know these waters well, then, Frederik? It looks to me like the only good anchorage is …"

"Whooo-heeee!!!" I yelled. "We're going to find a treasure!"

Neither Anna nor Frederik joined in my cheering. They were leaning shoulder to shoulder over the chart, talking about nautical things like bearings and currents and prevailing winds, with their heads so close together anyone would think they were the best of friends.

CHAPTER SEVEN

In which we look for treasure

few days later we were anchored by Serpent Island. Looking at the landscape, I could tell that the treasure was not going to be easy to find, even though the island was so small we could have rowed around it in a hour. It was a very steep island, like a black mountain that had fallen into the sea. Lush, dense jungle covered it, making curtains of green over even the steepest cliffs.

After a bit of arguing, Mister Flytch and Frederik agreed to row Anna, Yah-Yah, and me to the island. They would stay to guard the boat while the three of us went treasure-hunting.

"It's not that I don't trust you, Frederik," Anna protested, as we rowed along looking for the place her grandfather had told her to land. "Honestly. It's just—it was my grandfather's treasure and he wanted me to find it someday. I don't know whether he'd approve of giving it back to Queen Nevilla or not. I'm going to, but—I think I'd rather find it on my own, at least. For my grandfather."

"Of course," said Mister Flytch and Frederik.

"They'll follow us," Yah-Yah warned, with a little growl down in her chest. "You can't trust pirates."

"I thought you said he was sweet," I murmured in her ear.

"Frederik is sweet. But Flytch is a pirate."

"Even if he is," I pointed out, "he's retired. Besides, Anna's his captain and he wouldn't betray her. Hey, look at this, Yah-Yah."

I was peering over the side of the boat into the water. It was very deep; the island had no beach, but plunged almost straight into the sea. I couldn't see any bottom, even though we were only a few yards from shore, but I could see something. It was a snake, a yellow and black banded snake. It was twice as long as I was tall, and it was swimming through the salty water like an eel. Suddenly it saw the boat and darted away. Yah-Yah growled.

"Don't stick your hands in the water, Torrie," said Frederik. "There are a lot of poisonous sea snakes around here. That's why it's called Serpent Island."

"I thought you said the water was full of big fish."

"It is," he said. "The snakes have to eat something, don't they?"

I watched the snake swim away, a ribbon of yellow and black. It shot into a hole in the cliff just as Frederik shipped his oar and Anna stood up to fend us off from the rocks. We floated there, clinging to the cliff, looking up.

"Are you sure this is the right place, Captain?" asked Frederik.

"Yes," said Anna, and to me she added, "You see that streak

of white quartz up there, Torrie? At the top of the cliff? That's where we start."

"I can't climb that cliff!" wailed Yah-Yah. "I'm not a cat!"

"You'd better wait here, then," I told her. "You can guard the pirates, since you're so worried about them."

"No. I'm coming to look after Anna." The dog licked her lips and whined nervously. "You can pull me up on a rope."

In the end, we had to do just that.

Anna and I climbed up first, while Yah-Yah whined and Mister Flytch groaned and Frederik just plain covered his eyes. What you did was find a crack to work your fingers into, then find a lump or a crack to cling to with your toes. Then you looked for more rough bits to grab with one hand, then the other, and then you did the same for your feet. It was made harder by all the green ferns and vines that were draped from crevice to crevice. They weren't strong enough to hold on to, but they got in the way and tangled themselves around your arms and legs, and some sort of sticky-leafed thing got all through my fur until I thought I'd be stuck there forever, like a fly in a spider's web. Anna reached down and cut the sticky plant at its roots with her knife, while Frederik, who was peeking through his fingers, called to her to be careful. Then she almost fell off while putting the knife back in her belt. But she scrabbled with her feet and I caught her ankle and stuck her toe back in a crack, and then she could reach the top and pull herself over.

Yah-Yah howled the whole time we were hoisting her up to the clifftop. She said afterwards that she couldn't help it. I can't say that I blamed her. She had spun slowly around and around, banging now her muzzle, now her tail, on the rocks and prickly vines. It was enough to make anybody howl.

After Yah-Yah we pulled up a spade and my spear and Anna's sword and a picnic, and we set off into the jungle.

We didn't just charge blindly into the green darkness. Captain Lanius, when he was an old man sitting in a rocking chair with Anna on his knee, had shown her the island on a chart, and had made her memorize the way to find the treasure. We stood above the splash of white quartz in the black rock of the cliff, and Anna looked at her compass. She said, in that chanting way you say things that you've memorized, "East-southeast, giant stump." Then she looked ahead and found a spot that was east by southeast from where we were, and we walked to that, and found another landmark that was east by southeast, and so on, so that we always went in a straight line.

THAT SOUNDS EASY, but it wasn't. It was a real jungle. I could get through, being small and a forest creature, and Yah-Yah could get through most places, but Anna couldn't. Eventually what we did was, I would go to the next landmark Anna saw, so that she wouldn't have to worry about losing her straight line, and then she drew her grandfather's sword and hacked a way through all the tangled plants to me. Pretty soon we were all covered in sticky sap and the flies were buzzing around us, and Yah-Yah and I were spiky as porcupines. Anna's face and arms were all thorn-scratched and fly-bitten, her clothes were torn, and her hair had come out of its pigtail altogether to stand out around her shoulders in a fluffy, sticky, black cloud.

Sweat had run down Anna's face and front and back and stuck her shirt to her, and I was steaming, and Yah-Yah was panting, by the time we found the giant stump. It was just a big hummock of crumbly reddish soil now, with tall ferns growing out of it like a big headdress, but there it was.

"Treasure?" I asked.

Anna shook her head. We all had a drink out of the skin of water I was carrying.

"Due south, pink rock," she said.

We hacked and slashed and scrambled up a steep slope that was not quite a cliff. It seemed like miles and miles, although it wasn't, actually, before we reached the pink rock, halfway up.

"South-southeast," said Anna. "Red flowers."

That took us up the rest of the slope at a different angle, and along the top of a ridge of crumbly rock in which, joy of joys, very few large plants were growing, so it was easy to walk. Anna carried the spade over her shoulder with one hand and her sword in the other, and sang a treasure-hunting song:

> Hi-ho, treasure-ho,
> We're going to find a treasure,
> And then we'll give it all away.
> Hi-ho, whatever.

All right, I know it didn't rhyme. Anna was a master mariner, not a poet.

I wondered what would happen if it weren't the right time of year for the red flowers to be flowering. That would be the end of treasure-hunting. We would go back to the old plan of exchanging Frederik for Captain Icterus, and maybe the treasure would never be found and the Granite Isles would be blighted for ever.

"Red flowers!" cried Anna. "Time for lunch!" And she flopped down in the middle of them.

They weren't red flowers, really. They were some kind of plant that had a cluster of red leaves at the top of each branch, so they looked like flowers from a distance. We ate lunch and let the breeze up on top of the ridge cool us off and blow the flies away. Anna combed her hair out of her face with her fingers and tied it into a rather sap-sticky braid again.

Too soon, it was time to go.

"West-southwest, crater lake," said Anna, and off we went again.

Down off the ridge and into jungle again. On and on in the longest straight line yet. Horrible whining midges got in my ears and my nose. Down we went, down and down and down, steeper and steeper, and it wasn't just steep, but dangerous, with sudden holes and pits in the rock. Yah-Yah fell into one, disappearing with a yelp when the leaves she stepped on turned out to have no ground under them. It was a deep pit, full of big white spiders, which swarmed all over her in their hurry to get away, but luckily they didn't bother burrowing through her thick fur to bite. Once the spiders were gone I scrambled down and boosted her out, with Anna pulling from above. Yah-Yah danced around nipping at her flanks, and we had to pet her and soothe her for several minutes before she'd believe the spiders were gone.

After that we were more careful where we put our feet. I felt the way ahead with my spear, and Yah-Yah walked behind Anna. It was more like climbing down than walking. Or falling. We did a lot of falling. We couldn't see what lay below us at all, nothing but trees and ferns and creepers thick as fog.

Then, just when I was wishing I'd never thought of going treasure-hunting, my spear, which I was poking through some ferns, splashed.

Water.

"Water!" I shouted. "It's Crater Lake!"

At least I hoped it was.

"Water!" said Yah-Yah, and she pushed through the ferns to lap up a great mouthful. She spat it out the next instant.

"Ack!" she said, flapping her tongue around. "It's not a lake! It's the sea again."

"Yah-Yah says it's the sea!" I translated for Anna. She and I pushed through the ferns and tasted the water. Yah-Yah was right; it was salt. But it looked like a lake, or at least a pond. We were in a perfectly round basin, steep and green on all sides, and at the bottom was water, blue as the sky. In the middle of the pond was an island no bigger than a table, and on the island grew one huge tree rather like a giant mangrove or banyan, with its roots wrapped around and around the island like a basket.

"There must be an outlet to the ocean," said Anna.

"I saw a snake swim into a hole in the cliff," I reminded her. "Maybe it can swim through a tunnel and come out here."

"I hope not," said Yah-Yah, and she moved farther back from the water.

"Now what?" I asked.

"Tree," said Anna.

"Tree?" I asked.

"Tree," she repeated.

"What about all this east and south and east-east stuff? Is the tree the end of it?"

"Just 'tree,'" said Anna. "That's the final instruction. North coast: white quartz. East-southeast: giant stump. Due south: pink rock. South-southeast: red flowers. West-southwest: crater lake. Tree. That's how it goes. Grandfather used to sing it to me."

"Well, if I was going to call any one of these trees just 'tree,' I'd pick the one on the island," said Yah-Yah.

"They're all on the island," I said.

"That island," said Yah-Yah, pointing like a setter, with her nose and a lifted paw. "The island on the island."

I knew what she meant, of course. It was certainly the most impressive tree in sight. "Anna, Yah-Yah and I think it's that tree out there."

"So do I," said Anna, and we all looked at the huge tree with its snaking roots, out in the middle of the lake.

Anna tapped the end of her braid on her chin. "We could swim," she said doubtfully.

"Snakes!" yelped Yah-Yah and I together.

"Well, do you have any better suggestions? We can't carry the ship's boat up here through all that jungle."

"How did your grandfather get out to it?" I asked. "If he swam, it must be safe."

"Or else it isn't that tree at all," said Anna. "Here, what's this?"

She had been scuffling along the shore, and had kicked something.

"A root," I said.

"A rib," she said.

I yelped again.

"The rib of a boat, silly," said Anna. "I guess that proves it's the right tree. If someone dragged a boat up here, they must have been going to that tiny island."

It wasn't much of a boat. It wouldn't have held more than

one big person. But it was just the right size for one big strong person to have carried on his back through the jungle, if he was really determined to bring a boat to this puddle-sized lake. But it didn't do us any good; its planks had mostly rotted away. There were just a few curving ribs left, making a sort of boat skeleton under the leaves.

It gave Anna an idea, though.

"We'll make a raft," she said, drawing her sword.

I'm sure her grandfather wouldn't have approved of Anna using his sword to cut down trees. It wasn't good for the blade at all, and it had several notches by the time she had felled two middle-sized trees, hacked the branches off them, and cut each trunk in two again.

We should have brought an axe.

We lashed the four logs together with vines. It floated. First I stood on it, because I was the lightest, and then Yah-Yah joined me, and it still floated. Then Anna stepped carefully aboard. The raft settled in the water, so that every little ripple washed over our bare toes, but it didn't sink. I pushed off with my spear, and Anna paddled with the spade. The raft wallowed in the water, but it went slowly in the right direction.

Yah-Yah and I kept a close lookout for yellow and black sea snakes. All we saw were pale jellyfish, thousands and thousands all moving together one way, then another, like a cloud against the black depths. I didn't think there could be room in the lake for anything but jellyfish.

Finally the raft bumped against the island, or rather, against the tree roots. I jumped ashore and made it fast with a vine. Yah-Yah scrambled up onto the tree-covered island and sniffed around.

"Too bad treasures don't smell," she said. "I'd find it in no time."

"How big is it?" I asked. "Is it in a box or a jar or a chest?"

"I don't know," said Anna. "Hey, Torrie, come and look. All the jellyfish have disappeared."

I stared down into the empty water.

"Where did they go?"

"I don't know, but I know why they went." Something in Anna's voice made me look up again.

The raft was beginning to rock with waves that weren't made by the wind. There was something in the water, something sliding across just under the surface. It was yellow, and black, and a long line of ripples followed it. It lifted out of the water for a moment and looked at us with black, glittering eyes. Its forked black tongue flickered in and out, tasting the air, tasting sweaty young woman and unwashed dog and Old Thing on the breeze. A nice change from jellyfish, it was probably thinking.

It was a sea snake, and it was longer than *Shrike* and as big around as a cow.

CHAPTER EIGHT

In which we don't get eaten

You may think sea snakes, even giant ones, are not all that monstrous and exciting, but just wait until you see a sea snake that size swimming at you, and see what you think then. It was a real sea serpent, and even though I've faced dragons, I wasn't foolish enough not to be afraid of it.

"Get up in the tree, Torrie," said Anna, without looking back at me. She held her grandfather's sword ready, waiting for the serpent to strike.

I thought climbing up in the tree might be a good idea, but not for the reason you're thinking. The snake was lying under the surface of the water, you see. If I got up higher, I would have its whole long snaky body to throw my spear at.

Yah-Yah began to growl, a low, menacing growl. It started deep in her chest and came out very slowly, rattling my teeth. This was a serious growl. Even a wolf couldn't do better.

I climbed the tree and ran out on a good wide branch over the water.

Yah-Yah crouched.

Anna stayed where she was on the bobbing raft, so that she was between Yah-Yah and me and the snake, protecting us. She stood with her feet well apart, to keep her balance. She had no shield and no armor. Sailors don't like armor. It's hard to swim in. She held the sword in one hand and her knife in the other.

The snake looked at us. Its tongue flickered over its teeth.

And it struck.

It reared up out of the water and came crashing down on the raft, mouth open wide. Poisonous, Frederik had said. I hurled my spear and it sank deep into the thick body. Not good enough. I was a little out of practice since my dragon-hunting days (rats don't really count), and besides, the snake had twisted while it was in the air. I'd been aiming for its spine, which would have killed it. I missed by several inches.

Anna jumped out of the way as the snake came down. She swung and cut, and Yah-Yah darted in and bit and darted away, but Anna's sword was dull from chopping trees. Though the snake thrashed around in pain, a single blow wasn't going to be enough to kill it, even added to the wound from my spear, and neither was a dog bite. Anna pricked the monster on the chin with the knife as it struck at her again. It hesitated a moment, feeling the point of the blade on a tender spot, and she slashed again with the sword. The snake thrashed away, streaming thick blood. It disappeared into the cloudy red water, and Anna scrambled onto the island, panting.

"Quick," she said. "Let's find the treasure and get out of here. You stand guard, Yah-Yah. That thing's not dead yet."

"And it has my spear," I said sadly. Better my spear than Anna, but I'd had that spear for a very long time. I'd fought a dragon with it.

Anna began searching through all the little holes and pockets made by the coiling roots of the tree, and I climbed around in the tree itself, feeling in holes and old nests and the forks of branches. I found some nice warm eggs, but I didn't eat them because I felt sorry for the bird, having to live over a giant snake, and I found some big black crunchy beetles, which I did eat, because I never feel sorry for beetles and I was hungry again, but I didn't find any treasure. Neither did Anna. She didn't find anything to eat, either. Humans aren't all that keen on beetles, no matter how sweet and crunchy they are.

"We have to use our heads," said Anna at last. "There's a thousand places here where Grandfather Lanius could have hidden something small, and no place at all to hide anything large."

She thought a bit. "The tree would have been a little smaller back then, but not much. It's an ancient tree. Now, I'm Captain Lanius, and I want to hide something, and I don't want even my crew to know where I'm putting it. So I row over to the island and land here."

She went down to where the raft had landed. Yah-Yah kept an anxious eye on the surface of the lake, but it was smooth and still.

"And I come ashore." Anna swaggered ashore like a pirate captain. "I look around. I have something, and I want to put it someplace safe, so I can think about how I have it and Queen Nevilla doesn't and how I can come get it if I want it."

She frowned at the tree and at the ground.

"I'm the captain of the *Shrike*. I'm the terror of the South Seas. I don't climb trees. It's not dignified."

"Oh," I said, and I came down to the roots.

"I can't dig," Anna went on, looking at the spade we had used as a paddle. "This island's just a rock with roots over it. Nothing to dig. So, I stick whatever it is someplace that will be obvious to me if I come back."

Then she said, "Get up, Torrie," and she said it with such a scowl, still thinking like Captain Lanius, that I leapt in the air and halfway up the tree again. She had a sword in one hand, a knife in the other, and her hands were red with the blood of the snake. She looked like Captain Anna, the terror of the seas.

"Aha!" said Anna, sounding like herself again. "He'll have dropped it right down here." She abandoned her sword and knife and flung herself down on the roots, reaching into a hole right at the base of the tree, where it split into two of the biggest, oldest roots, and where I had been sitting.

"It's no good, Torrie," she said, after she had groped around for a minute. "My arm's too big. You try."

I came back down and felt where she showed me. I had to lie down on my side and reach in right up to my shoulder. It was like feeling around in a knot of frozen snakes, groping around under those roots, sticking my fingers into even the smallest cranny, because who knew what it was that Captain Lanius had taken. Well, Nevilla the pirate-queen probably knew, but she wasn't there. I didn't find any rings, or jewels, or necklaces. I didn't find any big masses of white spiders either, which made me very happy. But I did find something. It had a hard, circular edge. I thought it was a bracelet, but then I stretched just a bit farther, bracing my toes against Anna, to get ahold of it, and it wasn't.

It was a cup. A goblet, actually. Quite a big one. But the roots had grown in the forty years since Captain Lanius dropped it into the hole between the two biggest of them, and it wouldn't come out no matter how I twisted and turned and wriggled it. I gave up tugging at it and put my eye to the hole. In the spatters of sunlight that got down through the mesh of roots, the cup glittered like another sun.

"We'll have to cut some of the wood away," I said. "I can see it, but there's no way it's coming out."

"Right," said Anna. "I hate to do this. One dull blade is enough. But—watch your toes, Torrie."

She began whittling at the roots with her knife, shaving away the sweet-smelling wood, until we could squeeze the goblet out.

It was gold. It was covered all over, outside and inside, with finely engraved, spiraling lines of letters. Anna couldn't read the writing, and Yah-Yah couldn't read at all, and even I couldn't decipher the beautiful curling script, but the writing looked to me like one of the obscure magical languages sorcerers make up and use, to impress other sorcerers.

"It's beautiful," said Anna, rubbing her thumb over the pattern of spirals. "But is it really magic?"

"Oh, yes," I said. I'd have known the goblet was enchanted

even without the sorcerous writing. We Old Things can always recognize magic. Sometimes we might see a spell as light, or odd shadows. Sometimes it's a crackle in the air, like lightning or static in your fur. Sometimes it's a smell that doesn't quite belong. And sometimes, as with the goblet, magic is a sound.

"Can't you hear it?" I asked. I knew they couldn't, and yet it seemed incredible that they could be unaware of it.

"Hear what?"

"It's humming."

Anna held it to her ear. "I don't hear anything."

Yah-Yah cocked first one ear, then the other. "Neither do I," she said at last. "And I have very good ears."

"It's like the wind blowing through the strings of a harp," I told them. It made me think of my home in the Wild Forest, of deep green moss and shadowy trees with the summer wind in their leaves and the brooks burbling over rocks. I could have sat listening to it all day, but of course the others wanted to get back to Frederik and Mister Flytch. They were probably starting to worry about us, and it would soon be getting dark.

We put the goblet away in Anna's pack, which sadly had no food left in it at all. I cast off and Anna began paddling our raft back to shore with the spade.

"At least I found it," Anna said. "Grandfather would be proud of me for that, even if he wouldn't approve of giving it back to Nevilla."

"I still don't see how a cup can make the Granite Isles better," said Yah-Yah. "All you can do is drink out of it."

"We're just guessing about the curse," I said. "We'll see when we get there, I suppose. But it's certainly no ordinary goblet, I can tell you that. There's strong magic in it."

"I think—" Yah-Yah began to say, and then she barked suddenly.

I yelped. "Don't—" I started to say, with my hands over my ears. Then I saw what she saw.

"Take my knife, Torrie," said Anna. But it was steel, and you know what iron and steel do to us Old Things. Rashes and blisters. Ugh! I grabbed the spade from her instead. It had a nice safe wooden handle.

There were little waves beginning to bump against the raft, and ribbons of red were again discoloring the clear water.

Anna picked her sword up again and drew a deep breath. "Tie my pack to one of the logs," she said. "We don't want to lose the treasure now."

I tied the straps of the pack around one of the logs. I didn't like sticking my hands into the water, I can tell you. Then I picked up the spade again.

There was something moving on the surface of the lake: a stick, cutting through the water like a mast without a boat. It was the shaft of my spear. I decided I didn't need the spade.

The snake shot out of the water like an arrow.

"Yahhhh!" I yelled, and I flung myself towards the beast, grabbing my spear and spinning round it.

The snake fell and hit the raft just as Anna and Yah-Yah saw what was going to happen and dove off. The raft was smashed and disappeared, only to bob up again, slowly, one log, two, three, four, and a few bits of vine. The spade sank, never to be seen again.

Yah-Yah dog-paddled around the snake, growling, which was foolish of her as dogs aren't very agile in the water. One bite from the venomous sea-serpent and that would be that.

"Get away!" I shouted to her. "Get to shore. Go get help! We need crossbows!"

Yah-Yah hesitated, and then obeyed. Clinging to my spear, I tried to stand up on the snake's back. I couldn't see Anna anywhere. What if one of the logs had hit her on the head? I hoped Yah-Yah didn't think of that. We needed Mirimick the bow master and the rest of the pirates with crossbows. I got a grip on the snake's lashing back with my toes, braced myself, and yanked my spear free.

Then, holding my spear high over my shoulder, I ran along the serpent's back. It pitched and heaved worse than a frenzied horse or a ship in a hurricane as it thrashed around in the water, biting madly at the logs that used to be our raft.

"Anna!" I screamed. "Anna, where are you? Don't be dead!"

Anna burst up out of the water right under the snake's head. Sword first. Right into the snake's throat, just as I stabbed it behind the head.

The serpent's body jerked and snapped like a whip and I went flying into the water, still gripping my spear. Anna dove again and came up beside me. We swam to where the wreckage of our raft floated. I clung to the log that still had the pack containing the treasure tied to it. Anna held on to another with one arm, sword ready, just in case. But she didn't need it. We watched as the snake twitched and jerked. Finally, still and dead, it sank. Its blood made the water look inky black in the long shadows.

There was a lot of barking on shore. Yah-Yah couldn't possibly have run all the way to where Frederik and Mister Flytch were waiting and back again, but there they were, the dog, the prince, and the mate, all leaping out into the water.

Anna laughed and heaved herself up onto her log, sheathing her sword.

"Well," she said, waving to them cheerfully. "We've done all the hard work. We might as well let them have the fun of rescuing us."

So we floated there and let Frederik and Flytch tow us to shore.

FREDERIK AND MISTER FLYTCH, it turned out, had gotten tired of waiting for us, and had started worrying. Finally they had moored the boat and climbed up the cliff after us. Our trail was easy to follow, because of all the trampled and chopped plants. They had arrived at the lake in the crater just in time to meet the frantic Yah-Yah and to see Anna and I battling the serpent.

Mister Flytch was so upset about his captain almost getting eaten that he had to sit down, because of his shaking legs. Frederik was holding Anna so tightly her eyes bulged, but she didn't seem to mind.

"Hey," I said. "I was almost eaten, too." So the prince hugged me as well.

"What would Mirimick say if I let you get eaten by a snake,

dear? Didn't you think of that?" Mister Flytch asked weakly. Then he coughed and stood up again. "Enough is enough," he said. "No more treasure-hunting. I'm too old. My nerves won't take it. Captain, please, let's just rescue Captain Icterus, and then I'll go home and retire again."

"It's all right," said Anna, wringing out her hair. On me.

"Hey!" I said again, and wrung out my whiskers.

"Hey!" barked Yah-Yah, and then she shook herself violently. I shook myself back at her.

"Hey!" yelled all the humans, and the three of them went scrambling away. Fussy, fussy. They were already soaked, and it was Anna who'd started all the dripping on other people, anyway.

"What's all right?" asked Mister Flytch, and he shook his fist at me as, still dripping, I sidled up close again. "Don't you dare, you soggy furball!"

"We found the treasure," Anna said.

"It's just a cup," said Yah-Yah, but no one paid any attention. Of course, no one but me understood her, anyway.

Frederik and Mister Flytch clamored to see it, so we all sat down again, to let our nerves recover some more. Anna opened her pack and held up the golden goblet in the last light of the setting sun, to watch it glow red and amber.

And then she handed it to Frederik.

"Here," she said. "It's yours. Your Highness," she added, formally. "Give it to your mother, and tell her to give me my father back."

"And his ship, and his crew," Yah-Yah added, and I didn't

need to translate; her little whimper and her wide brown eyes did that. Frederik rubbed her head between her ears, to tell her everything would be fine.

"Thank you," the prince told Anna then, and he kissed her cheek, which made her scowl and turn bright red. But I noticed she hadn't tried to avoid it.

Yah-Yah frisked around, barking, "Captain Icterus is free, Captain Icterus is free!"

"Not yet," I said.

I was right to be cautious. Trading the cup for Captain Icterus and his crew sounded like a simple plan, but it wasn't that easy when we got to the Granite Isles. It never is, when you're dealing with pirates.

CHAPTER NINE

In which we aren't welcome

The sun was low in the sky, two days later, when we approached the entrance to the harbor on the largest of the three Granite Isles. We still had not decided the best way to win the freedom of Captain Icterus. Frederik insisted that once she discovered her son was alive, his mother would do anything he asked. And besides, he said, once the golden goblet, the great missing treasure, was back in the Isles, the pirate-queen would have no reason to keep Captain Icterus. When he said this he patted the linen bag he kept tied to his belt, with the cup in it. He never let it out of his sight—not that he didn't trust the pirates, or Anna. We all understood that he just thought it was far too important to his kingdom to risk losing.

The Granite Isles were very bleak, as Frederik had said. They looked like they were only the bones of hills and mountains, with dusty soil gathered in the valleys. It was as though a giant had swept them with a giant broom and missed the low places. There were trees with yellowish leaves and thin, yellowish grass holding the dust in place, but not very well. The city had once been white stucco, I could tell, but now the flat-roofed buildings were dreary gray. Even the setting sun couldn't cheer it up any.

There was hardly any wind, and what there was, was blowing offshore straight out of the harbor mouth, so we couldn't

sail in. We were passing by, looking for a good anchorage, when the lookout clinging to the top of the mainmast cried out, "Sail ho!"

In the harbor two ships had raised sail and were sweeping slowly, majestically, to intercept us, and on three more the sails were being raised.

"Um—" said Frederik. "Captain Anna? I think we're in trouble."

There was no doubt they were coming for us. They bristled with spears and archers, and the ship in the lead had a big catapult atop its forecastle. And these weren't cogs but galleys, with one big square sail and two banks of oars, or sweeps, and a nasty spiky ram for making holes in other ships. With all those oars, they didn't need to worry about wind. We did.

Frederik cupped his hands around his mouth and bellowed a sailor's bellow over the water.

"Ahoooyyy! It's meeeee! Freeederiiiik!"

I don't know if they didn't hear or if they thought it was a trick, but the only answer was a black rain of arrows, all of which fell short. They didn't have crossbows, just ordinary ones, thank goodness, or they might have skewered the prince and then what would Queen Nevilla have said?

"I think," said Mister Flytch, "that someone recognized old *Shrike*."

"It's nice to be remembered," said Mirimick, ordering her crossbow-men (and crossbow-women) up to the castles.

"Bother," Anna said. "I should have known better than to fly Grandfather's flag."

We all looked up to where the flag of the pirate Lanius boldly fluttered its skull and bird, telling everyone that *Shrike* was out of retirement.

"Whoops," said Mister Flytch.

"Show a white flag of truce," ordered Anna. "Let them know we want to talk."

"A white flag! *Shrike* doesn't fly a white flag!" Mister Flytch exclaimed. "Anyway," he added, "we don't have one, Captain dear."

"Then make one!"

"Out of what?" I could see Flytch really didn't like the idea of a white flag.

"Your shirt!"

"I'm wearing my shirt!"

"Your spare shirt."

"It's green."

"Get someone else's!"

"The prince is wearing Mirimick's," another pirate pointed out, not very helpfully.

"Flytch ...." Anna said, with a bit of a captain's growl in her voice. Flytch sighed and started off to do as she said, but by then Mirimick had taken care of it. She scampered nimbly up to the top of the forecastle, waving a mostly white nightgown on the end of a mop. The lead galley was closer now.

"Surrender your vessel!" the galley captain roared.

"It's me, Prince Frederik!" shouted Frederik. "We want to talk to the queen."

"Liar! The prince is dead! Heave to!"

"We want to talk to Queen Nevilla!" shouted Anna. "A truce! A parley!"

"Truce with *Shrike*? Never!" howled the galley captain, and a carefully aimed arrow ripped through Mirimick's blue-rosebud-spotted nightgown. "No parley with pirates! Surrender or be sunk!"

"Pirates!" yelped Yah-Yah. "Who are they calling pirates? They should talk!"

Mirimick dropped the mop and grabbed her bow again. "Do we attack, Captain?"

Anna hesitated. Frederik bit his lip, but all he said was, "These are my friends, too, my people." His brown eyes were sad and pleading. "That captain is my great-uncle."

"No," said Anna decisively. "We came here to negotiate, not to fight. We're badly outnumbered. We'll just lose the *Shrike* if we fight. Sometimes it's wiser to run away, and this is one of those times. We run."

She called to the pirate at the tiller to change course, and *Shrike* turned so that the wind was dead aft. Soon we were leaving the galleys behind, running with the breeze pushing every stitch of canvas we owned and the foam creaming under our prow. But they were shouting orders behind, and their sweeps were churning the water. With so many sailors rowing, a long, lean galley could still overtake us, unless the wind picked up. Galleys don't do so well in high seas.

Anna was thinking hard.

"If Queen Nevilla won't be reasonable, I'll rescue my father and his crew first, and then negotiate to get his ship back," she said. "She'll have to listen if I have her son, her hostages, *and* her treasure."

"Rescue how?" asked Flytch, with a regretful eye on the galleys. He would have liked to stay and fight, I could tell.

"We're still close enough to shore to swim," said Anna. "And it's getting dark."

"No!" said the mate. "Captain, it's too dangerous."

"There's no time to waste," said Anna. "Mister Mate, I'm going ashore to rescue Captain Icterus. Your orders are to lead the galleys out to sea. No fighting. I don't want you being foolish and heroic and getting yourselves killed or my ship sunk. Just lead them out and then get away. If you can't get away, surrender."

"Surrender! Think what your grandfather would say!"

With every minute we were farther from land. This was no time for them to be arguing, but I didn't like to interrupt.

"My grandfather," said Anna severely, "got us all into this mess. I'm the captain now, and I'll sort it out my way, Flytch."

"Aye aye, Captain," Mister Flytch said, duly chastened. "But you're still not jumping overboard. We're too far out. Your father doesn't like me anyway; what would he say if I let you be drowned?"

I didn't like all this talk of sinking and drowning, not at all. Lucky for them I, at least, still had my wits about me.

"A barrel," I said. "There's an empty pickle barrel in the hold. Bash the top on tight and heave it over. Then you'll have something to help you float."

"Brilliant!" said Anna.

"Yes," I said. "Thank you."

In no time at all the empty pickle barrel, with a rope tied around it so as to give a grip, was dropping over the side, and Anna without a second thought dove after it.

"Wait for me!" Yah-Yah whined. Her claws scratched for a hold on the smooth boards of the deck and with a grunt, she eluded Mister Flytch's grab at her, flinging herself after Anna.

"Oh no," I said, looking over the side. It seemed a very long way down. Anna and Yah-Yah and the pickle barrel were already falling astern.

Mister Flytch and the prince looked at one another.

"You are a prisoner," said the mate.

"It's a prisoner's duty to try to escape," Frederik pointed out, with a little smile.

"Well, hurry up about it," said Mister Flytch.

Frederik jumped.

"Someone," said Mister Flytch, turning a stern look on me, "has got to look after the young people. And I can't go, I have my orders."

I knew it was going to come to that. I sighed. And held my breath. And dove.

THE GALLEYS, SEEN FROM SEA LEVEL, were very, very large, and coming on very, very quickly. And all those sweeps hitting the water—I didn't want to end up under them. I began to swim, as fast as I could while using one hand to clutch my spear, towards the pickle barrel. The others were already bobbing beside it, clinging to the rope.

"What are you doing?" Anna was demanding of Frederik.

"Helping," said Frederik. "You don't know your way around the palace, do you? Well, then."

"Shh!" I said, although there was no chance of anyone on the galleys hearing us. "Come on. Swim."

"Well, you'd better not get any funny ideas about escaping," said Anna. "You're my prisoner until I have my father, his crew, his ship, and my ship back. And don't you forget it."

"No, sir," said Frederik, so meekly that he made Anna laugh, which was probably what he intended. "But we're going to get run over if we stay here."

We swam out of the path of the galleys, pushing our pickle barrel though the waves. Anna kept a good grip on Yah-Yah's thick ruff, since the dog couldn't hold on to the barrel. We were tossed around by the wash of the oars, but that was the worst of it. And no one shouted alarm. Night was falling very quickly, as it does in the tropics, and in all the long dark shadows we were invisible.

Keeping ourselves afloat with the barrel and kicking our feet together, we made it to land without getting too tired. It was black night by the time we stumbled onto the rocky shore near the harbor mouth. I sniffed the air and wrinkled my nose.

"Can you smell that?" I asked the humans.

Frederik sniffed. "It smells like home."

Anna sniffed. "Smells like land."

"Hmm. What about you, what do you smell?" I asked Yah-Yah.

Yah-Yah sniffed long and hard before she answered. "You, me, Anna, Frederik, salt water, washed-up seaweed, a dead crab that's too rotten to eat but might be nice to roll on, except Anna would get mad if I did, dusty stone, a herd of goats sleeping up on the hillside, donkey dung on the road into the city, and two cats walked by here an hour ago .... What do you smell?"

"I'm not sure," I admitted. The air was heavy with a strange scent, at once sour and bitter, like the breath of a sick beast. "I think it smells like ... magic gone bad."

"What is it?" Anna asked, since I was still sniffing. I told the humans what I had told Yah-Yah.

"What do you mean by magic gone bad?" asked Frederik. "Is it the curse? You can smell the curse?"

"Maybe."

"I didn't know magic had a smell." Anna sniffed again, as if she thought she might be able to detect it herself this time. "You said the cup was magic, and that it had a sound."

"Magic shows itself in lots of different ways," I explained. "Especially to us Old Things." Which was just another way of saying, "Maybe." I really couldn't tell what I was smelling, but I knew I didn't like it.

"Maybe it's just something rotting somewhere," Anna suggested. "Come on. We don't want to stand around here all night."

Creeping quietly along the dusty road, we made our way into the sleeping city.

Something rotten. If anything was rotten, I thought, it was the heart of the land itself. No, not rotten, but twisted, somehow. That made sense, if it was the curse. And I looked at Frederik walking ahead of me, with the cup bumping in its linen bag at his hip. Even from a yard or so away I could hear its music, a whispering, wandering melody. It didn't seem to be making any difference to the faint, rank odor in the air, though.

Maybe we were wrong, and the cup had nothing to do with the curse on the Isles at all.

With this heavy thought in my heart, I hurried after the others. At least the wind was blowing more strongly, and had changed direction a little. In a strong wind *Shrike* could easily outrun the galleys, I thought. I hoped.

≈≈≈≈≈

THE CAPITAL OF THE GRANITE ISLES looked like a nice city. In the middle of the market square there was a public fountain with a statue of some heroic ancestor of Frederik's, and most of the houses had window boxes full of flowers. The fountain wasn't fountaining, though, and the flowers were sad things, with brown edges to their petals and a yellow tint to their leaves. Still, you could tell the people were trying to be cheerful.

We got into the palace by climbing up a half-dead mango tree, carrying Yah-Yah. It was the same tree that Frederik climbed when he used to sneak out as a little boy, to escape his lessons by running wild in the mountains. Once inside, we crept carefully through dark, empty corridors. There was light in one room, though, and the door was a little ajar. The others hurried past quickly and were soon out of sight, but I looked in. No one would see me, after all, unless I wanted them to.

What I saw almost made me run after the others. Then I decided it would be more useful to stay and listen. I squeezed through the narrow opening and walked quietly in, invisible to human eyes.

It looked like a pleasant, comfortable room. There was an olive-oil lamp, like a little clay dish with a spout, burning on a big table, a big brass telescope pointing out the window at the dark sea, and a big red-cushioned chair. There was a portrait on the wall, showing a smiling boy with yellow hair and brown eyes. The frame of the portrait was draped in black velvet. It was a painting of Frederik, of course, and for a moment I felt sorry for the pirate-queen; she was also a mother who believed her only child was dead.

The room wasn't empty. A pale-haired woman with a thin, tired face was sitting in the big chair, her hands tightly gripping its arms.

Two men in leather jerkins stood in front of her, on the other side of the table. Both of them wore swords and tall boots. Between them stood a man who could only be Captain Icterus. He was tall, and almost as broad-shouldered as Mister Flytch. The black hair in his tidy pigtail was streaked with gray and so was his neat square beard. He was pale from being locked up indoors for too long, and his face looked thin and tired, just like the woman's. It was the face of someone who doesn't get quite enough to eat. His eyes were blue, like the sky above the sea, and very sad.

And the woman in the red-upholstered chair, of course, had to be Nevilla, the pirate-queen herself. Although she was wearing a thin gold band around her head as a very simple crown, she wasn't dressed very regally. She wore plain trousers and a leather jerkin herself, but I had known enough kings and queens to know that silk and velvet are only for grand occasions, and a pirate-queen, in particular, probably needs to be practical. Her face reminded me quite a lot of Frederik.

"*Shrike!*" she said, and she spat the word as though it tasted foul. "Don't tell me you don't know about this, Icterus. What's *Shrike* doing here? Who have you been plotting with? Who's commanding her?"

"I told you, I don't know, Your Grace," Captain Icterus said. "How could I? I've been enjoying your," and he bowed mockingly, "most kind hospitality for so many months now, how could I know about anything going on outside? I've never had anything to do with my father's crew, and the last I heard of them, they had gone fishing up in Erythroth. Are you sure your people aren't mistaken about the ship? Cogs are very common, after all. Some of them even have red sails."

"I know Captain Lanius's flag!" the queen snapped, flinging a hand out to point at the telescope, which I realized must be aimed at the harbor. "A shrike perched on a skull. Are you telling me my own eyes lie?"

Captain Icterus shrugged. "I don't know. I haven't seen this ship. I assure you, she's nothing to do with me."

The queen's eyes narrowed. "You're lying," she said. "Just like you lie about the treasure. And I've had enough of it. I've still got *Oriole* in the harbor, you know. I've been thinking I could trade her to some merchant from Callipepla for a few loads of rice or sell her for a decent bit of gold, but how about I burn her to the waterline instead? What do you think of that? Do you want to watch your precious ship burn?"

Captain Icterus's pale face grew even paler, and his hands clenched into fists. The two guards tensed, but then Icterus sighed and carefully unfolded his hands again. "Madam, I've told you and told you and I don't know how to make you believe me. It doesn't matter what you do. Keep me a prisoner the rest of my life. Keep my crew prisoner. Burn my ship. Kill me. It makes no difference. I cannot tell you where this supposed treasure of yours was hidden, because my father never told me. If it ever existed at all, he took the secret to the grave with him."

"He can't have!" Queen Nevilla cried, and I saw then what she feared, more than anything, was just that—that Captain Lanius had died without ever telling anyone where he had hidden her treasure. She had spent most of her reign watching her islands dying and she had lost her son and heir. She couldn't let herself believe Captain Icterus didn't know where the treasure was, because then her last reason for hope in the world would be gone.

Living with those sorts of feelings can make you a bit mad, I think. I really did pity her, then, and I thought Frederik was wrong after all. We shouldn't have gone treasure-hunting first. We should have brought him straight home to his mother, and worried about restoring the Granite Isles afterwards.

"I've sent agents to Erythroth," the queen said abruptly. "I've learned you have a daughter, Icterus. Once my people find her and bring her here, then maybe you'll be willing to tell me where your father hid my treasure. I can make her life very, very unpleasant, if I have to."

I stopped feeling sorry for Queen Nevilla then. Being miserable and hurt was no excuse for making other people miserable and hurting them.

Captain Icterus shrugged. "You may find Anna more difficult to catch than you expect," he said, but he was just putting a brave face on his sudden new fear.

"Phah!" said the queen, and jerked her head at the door.

"Come on, sir," said one of the guards, in quite a kind and friendly fashion, and the three of them walked out more like old comrades than a prisoner and his guards. I suppose they had done this fairly often, in the long months since Captain Icterus was captured.

The queen leaned forward with her arms folded on the table, resting her face on them. Then she jumped up, ripped the crown off her head, and hurled it at the wall, before she stamped out of the room. The draft from the slamming door blew out the lamp.

"Stupid!" I said aloud. I could have taken the pirate-queen herself prisoner, and I'd gone and missed my chance!

Chapter Ten

In which we don't quite escape

I t took me awhile to find Anna and Frederik and Yah-Yah again. I finally discovered them creeping along a dark corridor, with Yah-Yah in the lead, her nose pressed to the floor. It turned out they were looking for me.

"Where have you been!" the dog said with a surprised yip, as we met around a sudden corner.

"Torrie!" exclaimed Frederik in a whisper. "We thought you'd been captured!"

Anna just reached down and gave my hand a squeeze. "Where were you?" she asked. "We need to stick together."

"I've seen your father," I told her. "And your mother, Frederik."

"How did he look?" Anna and Yah-Yah asked together, and "How did she look?" demanded Frederik.

"Sad," I decided, which answered all three of them. "Nevilla just won't believe Captain Icterus, no matter what he says."

"Where is he?" Anna asked.

"I think they took him back to the dungeon."

Anna stamped her foot. "We were at the dungeon door when we realized you were lost, Torrie, you idiot. We probably just missed him."

"Well, if he's back in the dungeon, he isn't going anywhere," I pointed out reasonably. "That's the whole point of dungeons, after all."

Frederik looked thoughtful. He was probably fighting the urge to run off to find his mother.

"You should go," I told him. "We can find Captain Icterus ourselves. Your mother should see you."

He shook his head, with a grim, stubborn, princely look. "I said I'd help rescue Anna's father and *Oriole*'s crew, and I will. I can find my mother after." He smiled at me, a rather sad and forced smile. "She isn't going anywhere, either."

Sometimes there's no point arguing with princes, especially once they get ideas about duty and promises into their heads.

~~~~~

THE DOOR TO THE DUNGEON WAS BUILT OF DARK, heavy, nail-studded wood. It opened easily, and we went down a flight of broad stone stairs into darkness lit only by a few torches on the wall. Partway down was a landing, with a door opening onto it and yellow light spilling out. The humans crept past this door on their hands and knees, one at a time. Yah-Yah just scooted low, like a sheepdog circling a flock. When I got down to the landing I saw what they had seen. The door there opened onto a little room, where there was a guard, one of the two I had seen in Nevilla's study. I hoped that maybe the other one was off-duty now. It might take two men to march a sea captain through the palace and keep him from escaping, but it probably only took one to guard a bunch of sailors safely locked in cells.

He wasn't doing much guarding now. He had his chair tipped back against the wall, his boots on the table, and he was reading a book by the light of a lamp. The story must have been pretty good, because he hadn't noticed a thing. This often seems to happen to people who are fond of books. They just don't notice anything, not even escaping prisoners or burning cakes, once they start reading.

It seemed to me that Anna and Frederik were forgetting one vital thing about rescuing Captain Icterus. Luckily they had me with them, and I never forget anything.

I tiptoed, very, very quietly, into the guardroom. The guard didn't look up from his book. Of course, I was invisible to him. He had a big bunch of keys hanging on his belt.

I tiptoed right up beside his chair. I believe invisible burglars do this sort of thing all the time.

Holding my breath, I lifted the ring of keys from the hook on his belt.

Oh, my hands! The keys were iron, of course. My fingers felt as if they were burning. I held the keys against my chest fur, so they wouldn't clank or jangle, and very, very quietly, I tiptoed out again.

Oh, my chest! I just knew it was going to turn all red and itchy and prickly feeling, and then it would get blisters, and that would be worse. And maybe my fur would fall out and I would be bald and everyone would laugh.

But at least I had the keys.

I went on, down the stairs and along a lengthy corridor lined with doors. Each door had a little barred window in it. Anna was holding onto a big pale hand that was sticking out of one of these windows.

"Keys," Frederik was whispering. "My mother has keys, Anna, but I don't know where to find them. I thought you pirates knew about picking locks."

"My daughter is not a pirate," came Captain Icterus's voice in a whisper, at the same time as Anna said:

"Pirate! You should talk, Frederik! You're the only real pirate here!"

"Ahem!" I said, and I held the keys in the air and jingled them.

Yah-Yah let out a yelp of joy. I think the guard must have got to a good place in the book, because he didn't stir from his room.

The dog ran to take the ring of keys from me, and I was only too glad to let her have them, I can tell you. I stuck my iron-burned fingers in my mouth and sucked them. That's what comes of having adventures. You're always getting hurt and people expect you to be silent and heroic about it.

Meanwhile, Anna took the keys from Yah-Yah, wiped the slobber off them on her trouser leg, and unlocked the door of her father's cell. Her hands were shaking so that the keys sounded like sleigh bells.

"Shh!" I said, but then she had the door open. She and Captain Icterus rushed into one another's arms. Yah-Yah wound around their feet, whining her joy and wagging her tail until her whole body waggled. Then she couldn't stand it anymore and started jumping up on the captain, until he caught her in one big strong arm so that he was holding them both.

"Father!" said Anna. "Oh, Father!" And she wiped her tears on his threadbare coat.

Captain Icterus kept stroking her hair as though he couldn't believe Anna was really there, and his face was wet with tears, too.

"Anna, Anna, Anna!" he said. "I'd never have thought it. And Yah-Yah! How did you get here? You have to get away; it's not safe. And who is this?"

"Prince Frederik of the Granite Isles, sir," said Frederik, and bowed. "I apologize for my mother."

"He's my prisoner," said Anna. "You see, after the storm we had no water, so——"

"This is no time for telling stories," I interrupted, letting Icterus see me for the first time.

Captain Icterus looked at me. "What——?" he said, and then he blinked. "Who is that?"

"Torrie," I said, and bowed like Frederik. "Of the Wild Forest."

Anna's father tried hard not to look too astonished. He even gave me a polite little bow right back.

Frederik tried not to laugh as he took the keys from Anna to begin unlocking the other doors. They clanked in his hands, and the cell doors squeaked and groaned on their hinges as they were opened. The dozen sailors of the *Oriole* crept out, whispering together about how wonderful it was to see Anna again and how happy they were and all that. There didn't seem to be any other prisoners just then, no lords waiting to be ransomed or kidnapped princesses, but a dozen whispering, coughing, shushing, shuffling humans make a lot of noise.

Anyway, probably the guard had gotten to a slow part of his book. Or maybe he'd finished it. His shadow was coming down the stairs.

And then there he was behind the shadow, standing at the bottom of the stairs with his mouth open, the way you look when you've come to investigate a suspicious noise and found it isn't just rats after all.

He only looked stupefied for a moment. Then he drew his sword. He didn't seem to recognize Frederik, which was too bad, since that might have made things a lot easier for all of us, even the guard himself.

"Right," he said. "I'm sorry, Captain Icterus. I don't know how you and the others got out, but back in your cells, the lot of you."

Anna drew her grandfather's sword and stepped in front of her father. Yah-Yah growled.

"Get the prisoners out of here, Torrie," Anna said, never taking her eyes off the guard.

"No," I said, and, invisible to the guard, I went to stand beside her with my spear leveled at the man.

"Torrie! I'm your captain!"

"I never signed on as crew," I said. "And I never take orders."

"Torrie, please, get them away. If you don't, this whole voyage was for nothing. Father, go with Torrie, please!"

"No," said Captain Icterus, and he stood there with his fists raised, looking for a chance to thump the guard. "Get my crew away, you—er, Torrie."

"We're not going without you, Cap'n," said a sailor.

"Yes, you are."

"We're not, sir."

"There'll be more guards any minute. Get out of here!"

"Not without you, sir!"

This was getting ridiculous.

I didn't like it, but Anna usually knew what she was doing, so as the guard began to circle her and she turned, watching him, I took Captain Icterus's hand and tugged at it.

"Anna's the captain of this expedition," I said. "Come on. You should have seen her kill the sea serpent. With my help, of course."

"Sea serpent?" Captain Icterus groaned, but he must have realized that no one at all was going to leave if he didn't set an example, so he let me lead him, with the women and men of his crew hurrying after him. Frederik and Yah-Yah stayed behind with Anna.

"Get *Oriole*!" Anna called after us. "Go help *Shrike*! There are five galleys after her!"

Captain Icterus groaned again. "I knew it," he said. "As soon as Nevilla mentioned *Shrike*, I just knew it. I suppose that bandit Flytch is behind this?"

"It was my idea!" Anna called indignantly. "Get going, Father!"

I led them up the stairs and into the corridor. Behind us, swords rang together.

"Hurry!" I said, and started to run, pulling the captain along.

We raced through the palace, bare feet pattering and sea boots clattering on the floors. "Down the mango tree!" I said.

"Hurry. Anna won't come till she knows you're safe."

"She always was stubborn," said Captain Icterus, counting heads as his crew climbed down the tree. "Ten, eleven, twelve." He leaned out the window and called down, "*Oriole*'s probably still in the harbor. Do as my daughter said — go help *Shrike*."

"But sir!" protested a sailor.

"Do as you're told!"

And with that Captain Icterus turned and went running back the way we had come.

"Hey!" I shouted, racing after him, but I couldn't catch up and I think I took a wrong turn.

The floors were very slippery. I skidded around a corner and slid into the pirate-queen herself. We both went flying along on the polished floor, and when we got untangled we ran in opposite directions—she couldn't see me and she probably thought she had tripped. She was shouting, "Guards!" which I thought was probably a bad thing.

Down in the dungeon, swords were still clashing and clanging. Captain Icterus had gotten back before me, and he and Frederik were looking anxious. The prince had a soup bowl from one of the cells in his hands, but he couldn't get close enough to the guard to use it.

"Stay out of the way, Frederik," Anna said, as she parried a blow from the guard, spinning away just in time from a second stroke. Now she stood with her back to a doorpost. She gave me a look.

I knew at once what she wanted.

"Yarrgh!" I yelled, letting the guard see me, and I jumped at him from the side. Ducking under his sword, I used my spear like a quarter-staff, shoving him across the belly with its shaft.

He shrieked in terror, having no idea what sort of vicious monster I was, and Anna flipped the sword out of his hand as he stumbled and fell back.

Right into the cell.

Anna slammed the door, dropped her own sword, grabbed the keys from Frederik, and locked it.

"Hey!" shouted the guard. "Hey! Help! Help! *Help!* The prisoners are escaping!"

"Come on!" said Anna, and she snatched up her sword. "Let's get out of here!"

We all ran. Frederik stayed to shut the door at the top of the dungeon stairs, so no one would hear the hollering guard. But somehow Nevilla already knew there were intruders in the palace. In the distance I heard booted feet running, and voices shouting orders.

"This way," Anna said, and we all started to run, heading for our old friend, the mango tree.

We didn't make it.

CHAPTER ELEVEN

In which we *still* don't escape

On our way to the mango tree, we ran head-on into half a dozen soldiers, who were racing up the lamp-lit corridor towards us.

"There they are!" shouted the woman in charge. "Get Icterus, he's the important one!" She waved a stout stick in her hand. Obviously someone had realized that an escape was in progress and they had been given orders not to kill the man the queen still thought could lead her to her treasure.

"Sergeant, it's me!" Frederik called, but a young man can change a lot in two years on a desert island, and on top of that I think maybe the sergeant couldn't hear him over her own bellowing. Her stout stick thwacked him neatly on the shoulder and he went sprawling on the marble floor with a sort of a grunt.

I bit her in the leg, and she yelled and flailed around, trying to kick me off—I was invisible to her, which no doubt made her alarm that much worse. In her panic she whacked one of her own soldiers and knocked him down. Frederik grabbed that man's stick and, still on the floor, thrust it between another woman's boots and brought her crashing atop the one already groaning on the floor. Anna whirled, sword in hand, and struck a club away, and then kicked another man smartly on the knee. Captain Icterus and the last man circled one another, fists raised like boxers. We all watched as the soldier made a sudden jab with his left and then rapidly followed it with his right, but Anna's father just grinned and dodged back and forth before, with one solid blow to the chin, he laid the man out on the floor.

And the sergeant, who had been watching like the rest of us after having finally shaken me off, raised her stick, about to thump Captain Icterus from behind. Yah-Yah rose up from the floor like a leaping dolphin, trailing one long snarl instead of a plume of water, and seized her arm.

The woman yelled again and this time she dropped her stick. Yah-Yah's fangs were rather bigger than mine. But someone shouted in answer. More soldiers were coming. Yah-Yah let go and crouched protectively in front of Captain Icterus, making rather nasty smacking noises.

"Haven't these soldiers ever heard of soap?" she growled at me.

"Probably," I said. "But it's a hot country, and they've been running."

Actually, I had quite a bad taste in my mouth, too, but it didn't seem the right time to tell the soldiers they needed to take a bath.

"This way!" the sergeant screamed. "We've got them cornered."

This wasn't strictly true, as all her soldiers were groaning on the floor, but we could see it would become true very quickly if we didn't get out of there. Anna gave Frederik a hand and he heaved himself up.

"Which way?" she asked. Booted feet were drumming the floor both behind and ahead of us.

The prince looked around wildly, then lunged across the corridor. It was paneled in satiny red wood halfway up, and the upper part of the wall was beautifully painted with frescoes, which are paintings done right on the plaster while it's still wet. The scenes made it look like you were gazing out through a series of arches onto vineyards, where people wearing broad hats, and donkeys laden with baskets of grapes, were at work in the fields.

"White donkey, white donkey," he muttered, as he groped over the wall, but I was watching and I saw that what he was really doing didn't have anything to do with the painted donkeys. He was just making sure the guards were looking in the wrong place. With his big toe (we never had found any spare boots to fit him), he pressed a cleverly hidden latch down in the paneling and slid it sideways.

A square door, barely high enough for me, popped open.

"Quick!" Frederik called, and one after another we dove through it. He was the last, and as he pulled it shut behind him we were plunged into utter darkness. We could hear people thumping on the wall, and scratching noises as they tried to pry the door open again with their knives and the swords they hadn't dared use against us.

"We should be safe in here," Frederik said. "Even my mother doesn't know about this place."

"A secret passage?" asked Anna, as if she couldn't quite believe it.

"This palace was built by my great-grandfather," Frederik explained, "and he had quite a strange sense of humor. The passages were his idea of a joke, a mystery to tease his descendants with. There are rumors that there are a hundred of them, but I think only about twenty have ever been found. Some are just a hidden door between rooms, or a passage that goes a couple of feet and comes out in the same wall. I found three new ones, when I was a boy," he added proudly. "I never told my mother about them—they were useful for getting away from tutors."

"So where does this one go?" Captain Icterus asked.

"Upstairs."

"That's not a lot of help," Anna observed.

"It's better than straight back to the dungeons," Frederik said, sounding a bit hurt.

"Sorry," Anna said. "You're right. Let's get going. Which way? I can't see a thing."

My eyes had adjusted to the faintest of faint lights leaking in around the edges of the door so I could see, even if she couldn't, that the way to the right was a dead end. I crawled past them all and ordered, "Follow me."

The wall was starting to shake, as though the guards were beating or kicking it in their frustration. I hoped they didn't damage the frescoes. I moved quickly along the narrow passage, and soon it was dark enough that even I couldn't see. I stubbed my toe on a stair, and we started to climb. My feet stirred up great clouds of dust and my nose began to tickle. I could hear a snuffling sound that was Yah-Yah, doing what dogs do and trying to find her way with her nose. This, of course, was a very bad idea. Suddenly there was an enormous explosion of a sneeze right behind me, and I jumped into the air with a yelp, lost my footing, and tumbled back onto Yah-Yah, who kept right on sneezing.

We all jumped on the dog and tried to muffle her nose, which only made her whimper and struggle and stir up more dust.

"I hear them! This way!" we heard that same sergeant yelling, and boots clattered and the thumping on the wall started again beside us.

"Someone get an axe!" she roared, and a man said, "No way,

I'm not chopping holes in the queen's walls. We'd end up in the dungeons ourselves."

"Get going!" Frederik said, shoving at us all from behind, and we started scrambling up those steep and dusty stairs again. Pretty soon we went around a corner, and up some more stairs, and then we came to a sort of landing. There was no more passage after that.

Frederik pushed past me and felt around the wall until a latch clicked and another door, this one tall and very narrow, opened. He looked out cautiously, and then squeezed through. I held the door open for the others and had to laugh at them. The dark pigtails of Anna and her father were gray with dust, and Yah-Yah had cobwebs hanging from her bushy tail. We seemed to be in another corridor, this one paneled right to the ceiling with pale bleached wood.

"I'll make sure the coast is clear," Frederik said. "The rest of you wait here, and don't let that door shut."

"Why?" I asked guiltily, as it clicked behind me. I had only taken my hand away for a moment. It must have had a spring to pull it closed again.

"Because there's no latch to open it from this side," the prince answered. Then he looked back. "Torrie!"

"Sorry."

Anna had gone ahead and was peering around a corner, sword in hand. Now she came running back. "Soldiers!" she hissed. "Coming up the stairs. Where can we hide?"

"I don't know," Frederik said desperately. "Maybe —"

"I heard footsteps!" the sergeant's voice shouted. "Come on!"

I dug my spear into the fine crack in the paneling, trying to pry the door open again, and Captain Icterus came to help me. Yah-Yah gave my arm a quick nip. "This way!" she yelped. "Hurry!" She took off in a skittering of toenails, down the corridor, away from the direction of the sergeant's renewed shouting.

"Follow Yah-Yah!" I shouted, although I don't know why, since I didn't suppose she had any better idea than I did where we should go. Just at that moment, though, the dog seemed to be the only one acting decisively, and in a crisis, people just naturally follow the person in front. That way when things go wrong, it's all somebody else's fault.

Yah-Yah turned on her haunches like a warhorse and galloped up another flight of stairs. We pounded after her, and followed as she whirled around another corner and into what looked like a guest bedroom. It was empty; the pirate-queen's guests were more usually kept in her dungeon in those days.

"We'll be trapped here!" Frederik gasped, too late. Already my sharp ears could hear heavy boots coming up the last stairs.

"We could hide under the beds," I suggested, but I wasn't sure if Captain Icterus would fit under a bed. Maybe we could hide him in the wardrobe.

"Roof!" barked Yah-Yah, and even the humans understood.

"The roof!" Anna said. She heaved the window open and leaned out. Yes, it was the perfect place to get to the roof. Captain Icterus stood on the sill, reached, and pulled himself up. From there, he was able to help those of us who weren't quite so tall. Frederik came last, swinging up by the eaves and

kicking the window shut behind himself, so no one would guess where we had gone.

We all lay on the flat roof of the palace, safely hidden behind a low parapet, catching our breath. Down below in the palace we could hear boots running, doors slamming, men and women shouting, and the pirate-queen bellowing, "What do you mean, Icterus found a secret passage? Find him! And when I learn who let *Oriole* just sail away ..."

Frederik sighed.

"Poor Mum," he said. "I should go talk to her."

"You're still my prisoner," said Anna.

Frederik looked at her.

"Sorry," she said. "But now that we're trapped, I don't think I can let you go until we get off this island. We'll try to make it down to the harbor without being seen, but in case we are captured, I need you to bargain with."

"Once she has the treasure back, she'll probably let you all go anyway, Anna."

"You have the treasure?" asked Captain Icterus. "How? And what is this treasure, anyway? I knew my father said I should never, ever sail anywhere near the Granite Isles because the pirate-queen hated him and his whole family and I'd be in terrible danger, but I'd never heard of any treasure until Nevilla started asking me about it."

"It's a long story," I told him. "I'll tell you later."

Anna stretched out on her back with her hands behind her head, making herself comfortable. "You might as well tell it now, Torrie. I think we're going to have to stay up here until things quiet down in the palace."

So I did, and while I told the story of our adventures, we could hear the thumping of boots, up and down the stairs and corridors, in and out of rooms, as the pirate-queen's soldiers searched for us. I don't imagine anyone in the palace got any sleep.

The night was nearly over by the time I had finished.

"So," Captain Icterus said then. "The Isles are so barren and infertile because my father took this thing away?" He picked up the golden cup, which Frederik had taken out to show him. "Shouldn't something be happening to lift the curse, now that it's come back?"

That was what I had been wondering ever since we landed, but it was obviously the first time that any of the others had thought of it. They all looked at me, their eyes gleaming in the dim light that comes before dawn.

"You said you could smell the curse," Anna said. "Has it gone yet?"

"I said I could smell something," I corrected her. "It might be the curse, it might not." But I was fairly sure it was.

"Well, has it gone?"

I sniffed, just to be certain. It can be difficult to smell anything at all, when you're sitting beside a very furry dog who has been eating a lot of fish, hasn't had a bath recently, and is still slightly damp with seawater.

"No," I said sadly. "Whatever it is I smelled when we landed, I can still smell it now. It hasn't changed at all."

Frederik took the cup back from Captain Icterus and looked at it, frowning.

"Maybe this isn't the treasure," he said.

"It has to be," Anna protested, biting at the end of her braid again. "There wasn't anything else there on that little island. Was there, Torrie?"

"Nothing," I confirmed.

Frederik looked dejected. "Maybe I've been all wrong, and the treasure Lanius stole doesn't have anything to do with the curse after all."

"It must!" I said angrily. "The cup's obviously magical. It's not just the pirate-queen who thinks the curse started after Lanius stole something. Mirimick remembers the Isles being green and growing. She said it changed only after they stopped coming to the Isles. It would be just ridiculous if the two things weren't connected. It wouldn't be fair!"

But I knew perfectly well, magic didn't work itself out so as to be fair, and neither did adventures.

"Maybe we have to do something with it," Anna suggested. "Maybe it's not enough, just to bring it back."

"Do what?" Captain Icterus asked.

Frederik shook his head. The prince had no idea. Neither did I. If only some of my enchanter friends had been handy, we could have asked them to study the cup and figure out how it worked, but I didn't know an enchanter or sorceress closer than the borders of the Wild Forest, so that was no use. We were on our own.

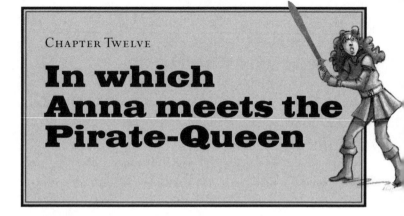

CHAPTER TWELVE

In which Anna meets the Pirate-Queen

After the sun came up the roof got hotter and hotter, even though it was still quite early. Think of lying on a rock in the sun. Think about the rock being hot, not just warm but hot, as if someone had built a fire inside it. Think of panting and panting and panting to get cool, and you can't; it just gets hotter and hotter and hotter. There's no water. Not even a little bit of damp mud, and you can't get off that rock and lie in the shade because there isn't any. That's what it was like.

I could get off, of course, because no one would see me. I was just going to crawl down, invisible, to raid the kitchens and bring back some water and breakfast for everyone, when Anna, who had been watching the harbor, called out softly:

"Sail-ho!"

"*Oriole*!" said Captain Icterus.

I looked over the parapet, to see a little white-sailed cog, with a slightly bigger red-sailed one following it. "And *Shrike*," I said.

"And the galleys!" said Frederik.

It was not what I would have expected to see at all; in the fair breeze, all seven ships were coming in together.

"They're not prisoners, anyway," Anna pointed out. "*Shrike* is still flying her own flag."

I wouldn't have expected to see that, either.

"I thought I told Mister Flytch to run away," said Anna.

"You did," I confirmed.

"I gave him an order."

"The thing you have to understand about Mister Flytch," I said wisely, "is that no matter how much he knows in his head that you're his captain now, in his heart, he feels you're more sort of an honorary granddaughter, and that he has to look after you."

Anna hung her head and groaned. "We need to get to our ships before Flytch does something really stupid, like storming the palace to rescue us. And before we all die of sunstroke. Torrie, maybe you could —"

"There goes my mother, down to the harbor," Frederik interrupted, before Anna could suggest anything.

"Good," said Anna. "Maybe now we can get off this roof."

"It's quieter inside, anyhow," said Yah-Yah, who was lying, panting desperately, in Captain Icterus's shadow, the only shade there was.

I agreed. "I haven't heard any stomping and banging for a little while. The guards must be done searching."

"There they go, with the queen," Captain Icterus said, and pointed to where Queen Nevilla was going down the street towards the harbor. A company of soldiers was marching behind her. She was dressed like her guards again, in trousers and boots and a leather jerkin, and this time she wore a sword.

We climbed off the roof and back into the palace, creeping through the almost deserted corridors and stairways to the window with the mango tree outside it. It was still very early and most of the palace servants weren't up yet. Probably they were all sleeping in, now that it was quiet. Only from the kitchens was there the clatter of people at work, and despite our growling stomachs, we kept well away from them.

Even though most of the palace had appeared to be asleep, the city itself was up. In spite of the early hour, everyone seemed to be hurrying towards the harbor. Some people were still in their nightshirts. The return of an ancient enemy like *Shrike* must be the sort of excitement people woke their neighbors up to see. We joined them, and found that no one paid any attention to us at all.

People gathered in the market with the heroic-ancestor statue in it, near the harbor. When we saw the fountain, every single one of us started to run. Yah-Yah reached it first; she had the most legs. We all plunged our faces into the big marble basin and drank, like—like people who'd spent too much time on a hot roof under a tropical sun. The water wasn't very good, being warm, green, and slimy. You could tell there hadn't been any fresh water running out of the fountain in a long time. I didn't care. Neither did any of the others.

Then I climbed up on the statue so I could see over the crowd. The heroic bronze ancestor looked a lot like Frederik, or what Frederik might look like when he was fifty, if he got to be very solemn and wise. He sat proudly on his horse with one arm raised in the air in an "on to victory" sort of way. I wondered if it was supposed to be the enchanter who had founded the kingdom of the Granite Isles, but I didn't have time to study it any more closely, because Anna tugged on my foot and ordered, "Tell us what's happening."

"The pirate-queen and her galley captains are about to meet," I called down. "And there are Mister Flytch and Mirimick, too, coming up from the wharves with the galley captains."

"Let me see," said Anna. Captain Icterus and Frederik made stirrups with their hands to toss her up behind the ancestor on the bronze horse. She stood there like a circus rider, shading her eyes with one hand, holding onto the ancestor's bronze hat with the other.

"They're talking," she said.

"They're arguing," I corrected.

"The pirate-queen is shaking her fist in the air," said Anna. "The galley captains are all looking down and scuffling their feet."

"Flytch is waving his hands around a lot," I said. "I can't hear what they're saying, though."

Anna let go of the bronze hat and cupped both hands around her mouth.

"Ahoooy!" she roared, like a sea captain trying to be heard over a hurricane. "Mister Flytch!"

The mate heard, and looked up over the heads of the crowd, and the pirate-queen heard, and the galley captains heard, and the soldiers heard. And they all began shouting at once, forcing their way through the crowd towards us.

"Are you sure that was wise, dear?" asked Captain Icterus.

Anna grinned. "Maybe not, but at least we'll find out what's going on." She drew her sword.

Standing on the rump of a bronze horse is not the best place to fight, so she jumped down onto the rim of the marble basin instead, as light on her feet as a dancer. I stayed where I was.

"No fighting," Frederik was saying anxiously. "Please, no fighting, Anna. She's my mother."

"You've done enough fighting for one visit," said Captain Icterus. "Let me have the sword."

"No one's going to need a sword," said Frederik loudly. "Put up, Anna." Something about the way he said it made us all remember he was a prince. He said it as if it had never crossed his mind that anyone would ever disobey him. Then he added, "Please?" because, after all, he wasn't Anna's prince.

Anna snorted, but she sheathed her sword. "I hope you know what you're doing."

"So do I," muttered the prince.

I kept a good hold on my spear, just in case. Yah-Yah began to growl, crouching at Captain Icterus's feet.

Queen Nevilla of the Granite Isles stepped out of the crowd, frowning. She might have been a handsome woman, but every time I'd seen her so far she was frowning or scowling or throwing things. That kind of behavior makes you look far from handsome.

"Icterus," she said. "And where do you think *you* are going?"

"I'm taking him home," said Anna.

"Oh, are you? And who are you?"

"My name is Anna. I'm master of the ship *Shrike*," said Anna, with her hand on the hilt of her grandfather's sword.

The queen looked at it.

"That's Lanius's sword," she said, and her frown got deeper. Then she looked at me and she didn't see me, and she looked at Yah-Yah and she sniffed, and she looked at Frederik.

She looked at Frederik again.

"Freddy!" she gasped. Her face turned gray and she swayed, and then she crumpled up in a heap.

"Mum!" shouted Frederik, and he forgot about being on Anna's side for a moment and went leaping to the queen. He pushed soldiers and galley captains out of the way and carried her over to the fountain.

While he held her, Captain Icterus dipped his handkerchief in the green water and gently wiped her face, just as if she hadn't been threatening to burn his ship and kidnap his daughter only a few hours before. After a moment Nevilla revived and struggled to her feet again, spitting algae out of her mouth.

"Freddy!" she cried, and hugged Frederik, which got him all green with algae, too.

While this joyful reunion was happening, Mister Flytch and Mirimick sidled through the soldiers until they joined us. Mister Flytch was careful to keep Anna in between himself and Captain Icterus.

"Ahem," said Anna, while Frederik was telling the pirate-queen all about being swept overboard in a hurricane and Torrie Island and what a wonderful captain Anna was.

They both looked at Anna. For a moment, the queen's face seemed to be glowing with happiness. She started to hold out a hand to Anna, still smiling.

Anna coughed. "Actually, ma'am, the prince is my hostage."

"What!" shouted the queen, and all the hard, angry lines returned to her face.

"Oh, er, yes," said Frederik. "I'm afraid so, Mum. The captain would like her father, his ship, and his crew set free. I'm her prisoner."

Nevilla looked Anna over from head to toe, and then from toe to head. There was no longer any gratitude in that look. I really think Anna could have chosen a better moment to remind the queen that they were enemies.

The queen's crown was on crooked. She straightened it. It was a bit dented. "Is that so?" she said. "It seems to me that you aren't going anywhere but my dungeons, so long as I have *Oriole* and *Shrike* in my harbor."

"Yes," said Anna, with a scowl at her first mate. "Exactly what were you thinking of, Flytch? Didn't I expressly tell you to run away?"

Mister Flytch rocked on his heels and looked up at the sky. "You didn't tell me where we were supposed to rendezvous, Captain," he said. "I came back for orders."

"For orders!" she spluttered.

"Your Grace!" shouted a galley captain who looked even older than the pirates. "Flytch said he had the treasure, Your Grace! Lanius's treasure! He said he'd throw it overboard if we didn't give him safe passage into the harbor to meet his captain!"

Frederik opened his mouth, and then he caught the imploring look in Anna's eyes. He hesitated, then backed a little away from his mother, fumbling at the strings that held the linen bag with the cup in it to his belt. When he had it untied he reached up over his shoulder, handing the bag to me with a wink. Then he folded his arms across his chest.

I had no idea what his plan was, if he had one, or what he expected me to do with the treasure.

"They did rescue me, Mum," he said. "There's no need for us to fight."

But the pirate-queen was staring at Mister Flytch in horror.

"You wouldn't dare!" She turned to the galley captain. "He didn't, did he, Uncle? He didn't throw the treasure overboard? Where is it? Does he really have it?"

Mister Flytch held up a linen sack a lot like the one Frederik had just given me. I think they'd had sugar in them, once. When Nevilla lunged at it he jumped back.

"Not a chance, Nevilla, darling," he said. "You give me your word, as an old friend and an honest pirate, that you'll let all the folk of *Shrike* and *Oriole* go, and then you can have this."

Anna shook her head at Mister Flytch, but he ignored her, grinning at the queen. I agreed with Anna. Trying to trick the queen was a really bad idea. No one would believe a promise made in response to a trick had to be kept.

But Flytch had been a pirate for most of his life. It was in his nature, when dealing with an enemy, to try tricks and double-crosses to make sure he came out on top in the end, and I guess at his age he wasn't going to outgrow it.

Queen Nevilla ground her teeth.

"Fine," she snapped. "They can go, once I have the treasure."

"They go first, and we'll leave the treasure floating in a barrel for you to pick up," Flytch countered.

"I don't think —" Captain Icterus began to say, just as Anna started to say, "That's enough, Mister Flytch —" but neither of them got to finish.

Queen Nevilla drew her sword and lunged at Flytch. He dodged away, but that was what she had expected. In the moment his eyes were on her blade and his right hand reaching for the hilt of his own, her other hand snatched and she sprang back with a triumphant cry, holding up the linen bag. In the space of a heartbeat she shoved her sword back into her belt and plunged her hand into the sack, coming out holding up—a very lumpy potato.

"Time to go," said Flytch. "Run, Captain!"

Guards knocked him and Mirimick to the ground as they tried to flee. The rest of us didn't have a chance to move.

With a howl of rage, the queen drew her sword again and swung around towards Anna.

CHAPTER THIRTEEN

In which I save the day

Anna moved just as swiftly. Her own sword flashed out and she shoved her father behind her as she blocked the queen's blow.

"Anna!" Frederik screamed, and more than anything, it was the fact that it was Anna's name he screamed that shocked Queen Nevilla into holding her temper for a moment. "Mum!" he said then, as she looked over at him, and his voice shook. "Don't! I—the captain is my—my rescuer. My *friend*."

In that moment I'd had my spear aimed to cast at the queen. Even if it meant killing her, even if she was Frederik's mother, I'd have done it to save Anna's life. But Anna had been fast enough to save her own, and the pirate-queen, I was interested to see, looked rather ashamed of herself.

It's a very bad thing to lose your temper so utterly, when you have a weapon in your hand. True warriors know this.

"Where is the treasure?" the queen demanded, through clenched teeth.

"I gave it to Prince Frederik as soon as I found it," Anna said innocently. "After all, he has a far better right to it than me, and he's … well, I knew he'd do what was right, for everybody."

"Freddy?" the queen asked, and her face lit up. "You mean you have it?"

"*Frederik*," Frederik muttered under his breath. "Well, I don't have it on me," he went on truthfully. "It's in a safe place, Mum, don't worry. I think, though, that I'll wait until *Shrike* and *Oriole* have left before I get it. There are too many short tempers here, and too many people with bad memories of one another, and … I don't want to see your temper make you do something that would make me think worse of you. You've never been reasonable where the treasure's concerned. So they go first, and then I'll get the treasure."

Frederik raised his eyebrows at me where I perched on top of the statue in the middle of the marble fountain, invisible to Queen Nevilla and her people.

Ah! I understood. Frederik wanted me to leave the bag with the treasure in it up there. He could climb up and fetch it down after we'd left safely.

But I could still smell the sick, sour odor of the cursed land. What would happen to the prince, I wondered, if it turned out to be the wrong treasure, after all? Would his mother blame him? He might end up in his mother's dungeons himself, no matter how glad she seemed to have him back now.

I could still hear the music of the enchanted golden goblet, like the strings of a clear harp.

It was louder than it had been on Serpent Isle or even down by the harbor last night, when we first landed on the island and I smelled the curse. In fact, it was growing even louder yet. The goblet was making a noise like a dozen harps sitting on a windy hilltop, with two dozen silver bells thrown in, all ringing very sweetly and loudly. It was beautiful, but it made it hard for me to concentrate on anything else.

It was a strong, strong magic. It was starting to make my skin itch, not in a bad way, but in that sort of excited way that makes you want to stretch and yell and jump around, like the first warm wind of spring when all the brooks are overflowing their banks and little streams go leaping down the hillsides, turning stony paths into waterfalls. That sort of feeling.

I looked at the statue of Frederik's heroic ancestor. There was no doubt in my mind any more. The statue had to be the enchanter-king who'd led his loyal people to these barren islands and turned them into a green paradise. I looked at the way he had his hand flung up, like a commander beckoning his armies on, and I thought, a knight or a king would usually be holding a sword, and his hand is empty. I looked at how the bronze hand curved, as if it ought to be holding something.

I took the golden goblet out and dropped the bag. The wind caught it and it floated down to the cobbled market square. Some people watched the sack, wondering where it had come from, but most people were watching Queen Nevilla arguing with her son.

"Are you saying you don't trust me?" she was demanding.

"I want to trust you, Mum," Frederik said. "But you've been a pirate so long, sometimes I wonder if you've forgotten how to be a queen. And I won't risk the lives of people I care about on something I can't control, like your temper. I'm sorry." He said this very firmly, but I saw how miserable his eyes were.

The queen just stood there, looking stunned. This couldn't be the way she'd imagined things going, when she had dreamed, as she must have dreamed, of Frederik coming home.

"I'm sorry, Mum," Frederik said again, and his voice did shake, this time. Anna put her hand comfortingly on his shoulder.

Queen Nevilla looked at them standing there together. Then she looked down at her feet. "Your friends can go," she said quietly. "You're right, Freddy. I'm sorry."

I looked away from the prince and his mother. Both their faces hurt too much.

The golden goblet was growing cold in my hand, cold like mountain water just melting off the high snows, and its music was like silver and crystal. Water, I thought. It wants water. I knew it as certainly as if I'd heard the cup's own voice in my mind.

I slid down off the bronze statue and dipped the goblet, letting it fill with green, algae-thick water from the marble basin. I climbed the heroic statue again, with algae dripping down my arm and into my fur. I was shivering all over, my whole body thrumming to the music of the goblet.

Anna, Yah-Yah, Captain Icterus, and Mister Flytch and Mirimick, now being helped up by the soldiers, all watched. Frederik stopped arguing with his mother. His eyes followed

me. I was aware of all of them watching, but I didn't realize the humming goblet had made me visible to the whole market square, until Queen Nevilla whispered, "The treasure … that brownie has the treasure."

I felt as though everything and everyone around the fountain was very far away in some remote dream. I'd never have let her get away with calling me a brownie otherwise.

Trying not to spill any of the greasy green water from the brimming goblet, I climbed up onto the heroic ancestor's bronze hat, and stretched up as high as I could reach along his arm.

I'm sure that the bronze hand actually moved, clasping its fingers around the stem of the goblet again. All the bells and harps that only I could hear played one great resounding chord and fell silent.

"Where did that creature come from, and how did it get

my treasure?" Queen Nevilla asked, in a more ordinary voice, pointing at me.

"What happens now, Torrie?" Frederik asked ... but then water dripped from the goblet.

Drip. Drip drip. Dripdripdrip, into the slimy basin. Everyone stared and was silent. Clear water, a sparkling stream of it.

I realized that the sour, bitter smell that had been burning my nostrils ever since I landed on the Isles was disappearing, growing fainter and fainter. I could almost see waves of the fresh scent of pure water rippling out from the fountain, rolling over this island, and flowing over the other two until all three of the Granite Isles were washed clean by them.

A murmuring began to run through the crowd. Every person whispered to the next, excited, happy. They pushed closer and closer to the fountain, looking at the stream that was filling the basin and running away down a channel in the street, washing the algae out to sea. The water chimed like bells over the stones.

Queen Nevilla pulled Frederik to her and kissed his cheek, laughing and crying at once.

Captain Icterus took Anna's hand and jerked his chin towards the harbor. Anna raised an eyebrow at Mister Flytch and Mirimick, winked at me, and nodded. Yah-Yah was already threading a way through the crowd that was pressing in around the fountain, those nearest shouting back to the ones farthest away to come and look at the water. It's amazing how quickly you can get through a solid mass of people, if you have good sharp teeth to give their calves a little nip. I slid down the flank of the bronze horse and waded through the water, scooping up a few mouthfuls as I went. Good, sweet water, cold and crisp.

The Granite Islanders didn't pay any attention to us, even to me. They were too busy marveling at the fountain.

"So that cup really *was* the treasure," Mirimick remarked, as we hurried along the cobbled street to the wharves where *Shrike* and *Oriole* were tied up. "I remember it now. I'd never have recognized it, though. The goblet I remember the statue holding was all crusty with minerals. It looked like it was made out of stone back then. Lanius must have polished it up."

"If only the queen had just listened to me," Captain Icterus said. "And if I'd known Anna knew where the treasure was all along, we'd have been happy to get it back for her."

"It all comes of having pirates in the family," said Yah-Yah. "They're nothing but trouble."

I decided not to translate that remark.

"What I don't understand," Anna said, "is why my grand-father didn't dig it up and sell it long ago. It almost seems as though he knew what the treasure did all along, and blighted the islands on purpose."

"Um——" said Mister Flytch. He looked at Captain Icterus, and then he shrugged. "It's all ancient history now."

"Revenge," said Mirimick sadly. "It must have been revenge. Nevilla wasn't the only one with a nasty temper, you know. Lanius never did like to lose."

"We used to come here all the time," said Mister Flytch. "You see, Anna dear, your grandfather was courting Nevilla, back in those days—that was after your poor mother died, Captain Icterus."

Mirimick nodded. "Queen Nevilla didn't discourage him, not at first, even though he was a fair bit older than her." She sighed. "Lanius was so handsome, even when he was getting to be middle-aged, which he was, then. After a while Queen Nevilla decided she didn't want to marry a pirate, and Lanius wouldn't reform. He was so mad when she told him. The names he called her … well, that's all water under the bridge, over and done with now. So we robbed the palace one night, to get back at her for breaking his heart, he said. I suppose she'd told him what the goblet did, back when she was thinking of marrying him. Foolish of her, but we're all foolish when we're young. He must have grabbed it from the fountain on the way back to the harbor, just for revenge."

Flytch shook his head. "No wonder he never told us. Pirates or not, we wouldn't have put up with that. Tormenting a whole kingdom that way!"

"I loved him dearly," Captain Icterus said. "But once he decided someone was an enemy, my father was not a very nice person. And he always had to get his own way. I'm glad we were able to undo the damage he did here."

"We?" I asked.

Icterus laughed. "Alright. *You*, Torrie."

"It took all of us to get the treasure here," Anna said, ruffling up the fur on my head as if I were Yah-Yah.

At the harbor we separated to go to our ships. Captain Anna and Captain Icterus stood for a moment clasping hands, and he kissed the top of her head. "Safe voyage, dear," he wished her.

"CAST OFF!" called Captain Anna on *Shrike*, and "Cast off!" called Captain Icterus on *Oriole*. There were no enemies to hear. Even the crews of the galleys had all gone streaming up into the city to see the wonderful fountain.

"Ahoy!" shouted one forlorn voice on the wharf. "You're not going now?"

"Yes, we are," Anna called back to Frederik, as the crew coiled the mooring lines and pushed us away from the wharf. "We're going while the going's good."

"But you don't have to. Really. Everything will be better now, just wait and see. She'll give up piracy. The Isles will be green again. Wait and see." Frederik leapt over the widening gap between the wharf and *Shrike*, to land on our deck. The pirates who were raising the yard on the mizzenmast stopped what they were doing and with no sail to catch the gentle breeze, *Shrike* just hovered where she was, bobbing gently. Both *Oriole*'s sails were climbing the masts, though, and Captain Icterus's ship was heading towards the harbor mouth. In the short time since we had sat on the palace roof and watched the ships return, the wind had swung round to blow off the land, making our escape easier—at least if we didn't linger too long saying our farewells.

"Good-bye, Frederik!" Yah-Yah barked from atop the forecastle of *Oriole*. Her barking made Anna's father look around. When he saw that *Shrike* still didn't have her sails set, he called out orders and the *Oriole* turned, spilling wind from her own sails, waiting to see if we needed help.

Anna didn't notice. She shook her head. "I can't risk staying. What if your mother's used to being a pirate? How would I make a living if she kept *Shrike*? I'm a merchant captain. I need my ship."

Mirimick sighed. "You hear that, Flytch, old boy? We're merchants now."

"Respectable." Flytch sighed too. "Still, it's more interesting than fishing."

But Anna and Frederik were ignoring them. "Mum won't keep your ship," Frederik assured her. "She said you could all go, remember?"

"And we're going."

"But —" Frederik's ears turned red. "I thought … I don't want you to go. Not like this."

"We'll come back," I said. "I'll make sure of it." And I gave Anna a stern look. She was frowning down at her own feet and didn't notice.

"I'll miss you," she said at last.

"Then stay."

"I can't."

"I don't mean stay here in the city. I know what your ship means to you. I mean, why not make the Granite Isles *Shrike*'s home port? Everyone needs a place to come home to."

"That's a good idea," Mirimick said. "It's not like we'll miss Queen's Harbor. It was too cold in the winter for my old joints, and they didn't even like us very much there."

"It's true they don't like us very much here, either …" Mister

Flytch said. I gave him a little kick on the ankle. I didn't think the pirates' comments were helping any.

Anna looked up, frowning and tapping her teeth with her pigtail. Then suddenly she grinned, flipping her braid back over her shoulder. "A home port," she said. "I'd like that. But what about your mother? I can just see it. *Shrike* sails into the harbor, we're all happy to be here, and next thing we know we're in the dungeons eating seaweed soup and rice."

Frederik shrugged. "I'd come and visit you there, of course," he said, with a teasing smile. "But Torrie could probably rescue you."

"Well, of course. But it might be you we had to hit over the head with a soup bowl."

"Will you trust me?" Frederik asked. "I give you my word, my mother won't do anything to harm you, if you come back. When you come back."

Anna looked very serious again. After a long moment she said, "Yes."

Frederik looked much happier. "Well, that's alright, then," he said. "So, Captain, where are you sailing to?"

"I haven't decided," Anna said. "I need to pick up a cargo somewhere."

"I was thinking," Frederik said, looking up at the sky, "that I need to hire a sea captain to bring me a load of seedling trees. So I can start replanting the forests."

"Trees?" Anna said, and she smiled so her dimples showed. "I could probably be hired to carry trees. They're not nearly as smelly as salt fish."

"Oh!" I said, hopping from one foot to another in my excitement. My feet were getting that itchy, adventurous feeling again. "I know just where we can go."

"Where?" they both asked.

"The Great Southern Continent!" I said. "Think of the trees we could bring you from there, Frederik. Maybe even things no one here has ever seen before!"

Anna laughed. "Why not?"

"Why not?" Frederik agreed. He looked a little wistful. "I wish I could come with you, but it wouldn't be fair to my mother to leave again so soon. And anyway, she'll need me here. I expect I'll be spending a lot of time making official apologies to the mainland kingdoms for our piracy. I'll have to, if we're going to be an honest kingdom again."

"So that's settled, then?" Anna asked.

"You can consider yourself hired, Captain," Frederik said.

"Trees it is, Your Highness," Anna said, with as grand and courtly a bow as I had ever managed. Then she leaned forward and gave Frederik a quick kiss. Actually, it wasn't all that quick.

"All ashore what's going ashore!" sang out Mirimick. We were drifting away with the outgoing tide.

"I'll expect you back with my trees before the rainy season!" Frederik called, and he made a great flying leap to the tarry timbers of the wharf. "Safe voyage, *Shrike*!" he wished us all. "Look after one another!"

"You keep your mother honest!" Anna called back to him, and then she started shouting at her crew. "What are you all looking at? Get those sails up!"

The white lateen sail and the red mainsail went up, snapping in the strengthening breeze, and the bird and skull flag of Captain Lanius whipped out from the masthead. As soon as *Oriole* saw we were under way, Captain Icterus waved at us and at Frederik, and the other cog turned, gathering the wind in her own sails. We slipped away out of the harbor together and left the Granite Isles falling slowly astern. Frederik stood on the wharf waving until he was just a faint, pale speck. When I looked through Anna's telescope, I could see the pirate-queen standing beside him with her arm around his shoulders. They both looked quite happy.

AND THAT, MORE OR LESS, was the end of that adventure. We sailed along with *Oriole* for a while, but when Captain Icterus went off to Callipepla to deliver his cargo of woolen cloth, which the pirate-queen had never gotten around to selling after he was captured, Anna plotted a course for the city of Keastipol in the Great Southern Continent. Eventually, we did return to the Granite Isles, and Frederik did get his trees—eucalypts and sweet flowering wattle trees and tree ferns and bunyas, which have dark green needles like daggers and cones so big they can kill you if they fall on your head. The forests of the Isles became one of the wonders of the world.

Anna and the old pirates did make the Granite Isles their home, the place they came back to after every voyage, and Captain Icterus and Yah-Yah visited whenever *Oriole* was in the neighborhood. Anna became the admiral of the Isles' great trading fleet, and Frederik, after his mother retired from ruling and went to sea again herself—we don't know *for certain* that she went back to piracy—became known as the Planter King. And in time, Anna and Frederik were married, and some of their children went to sea, and some of them loved the mountains and the forests, and they all spent a lot of time hunting for secret passages in the palace with Yah-Yah's pups and grandpups.

But as for what happened on the Great Southern Continent while I was hunting for exotic trees for Frederik ... well, it was an adventure, just as I thought. But that's another story.